RISE OF THE
TEENAGE MUTANT NINJA
TURLES

™

THE BIG REVEAL

Become our fan on Facebook facebook.com/idwpublishing
Follow us on Twitter @idwpublishing
Subscribe to us on YouTube youtube.com/idwpublishing
See what's new on Tumblr tumblr.idwpublishing.com
Check us out on Instagram instagram.com/idwpublishing

IDW

nickelodeon

Collection Edits
JUSTIN EISINGER
and ALONZO SIMON

Collection Design
CHRISTA MIESNER

Cover Art
CHAD THOMAS

Chris Ryall, President and Publisher/CCO
John Barber, Editor-In-Chief
Cara Morrison, Chief Financial Officer
Matt Ruzicka, Chief Accounting Officer
David Hedgecock, Associate Publisher
Jerry Bennington, VP of New Product Development
Lorelei Bunjes, VP of Digital Services
Justin Eisinger, Editorial Director, Graphic Novels & Collections
Eric Moss, Senior Director, Licensing and Business Development

Ted Adams and Robbie Robbins, IDW Founders

ISBN: 978-1-68405-530-2   22 21 20 19   1 2 3 4

Originally published as RISE OF THE TEENAGE MUTANT NINJA TURTLES issues #3-5.

Special thanks Joan Hilty and Linda Lee for their invaluable assistance.

For international rights, contact licensing@idwpublishing.com

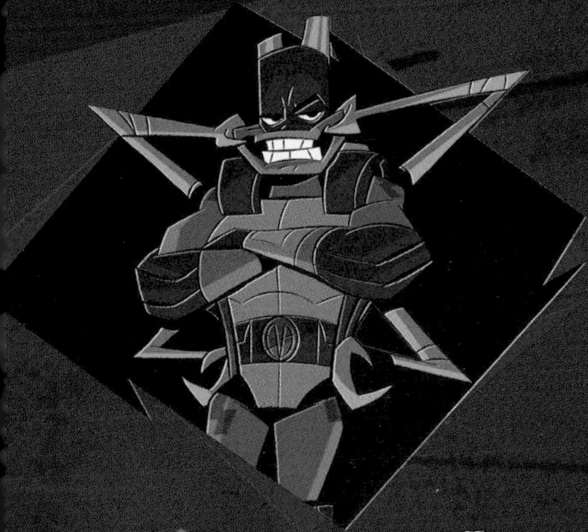

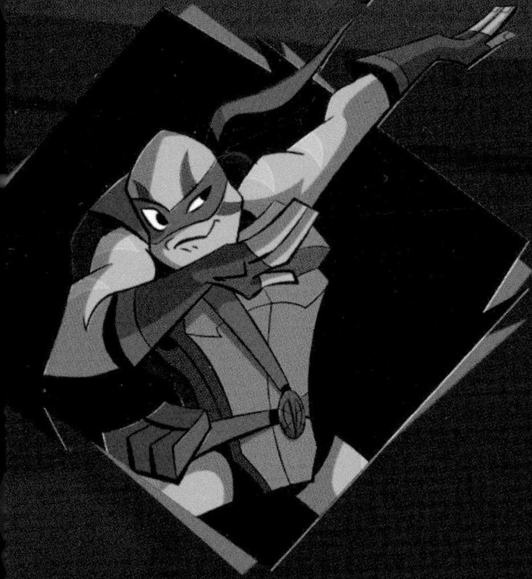

WRITTEN BY

MATTHEW K. MANNING

ART BY

CHAD THOMAS

COLORS BY

HEATHER BRECKEL

LETTERS BY

CHRISTA MIESNER

SERIES ASSISTANT EDITS BY

MEGAN BROWN

SERIES EDITS BY

BOBBY CURNOW

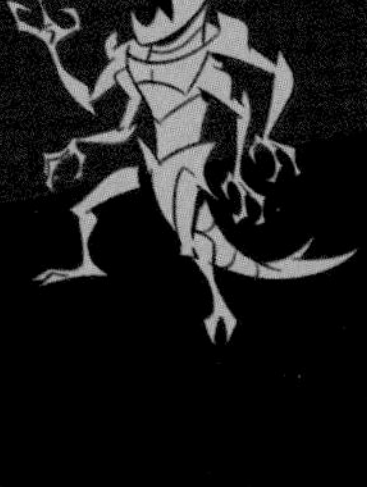

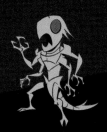

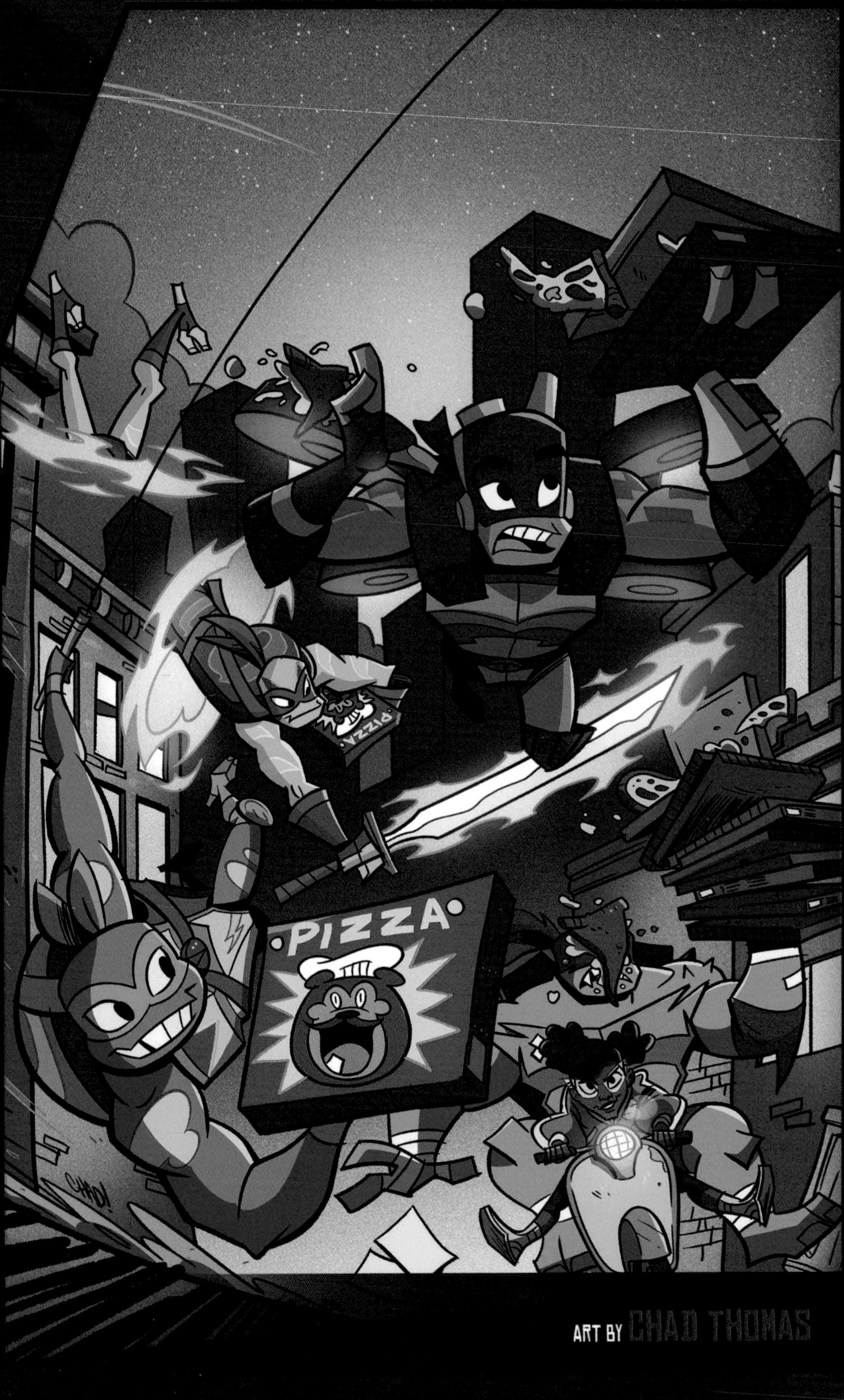
PIZZA
PIZZA
CHAD!

ART BY CHAD THOMAS

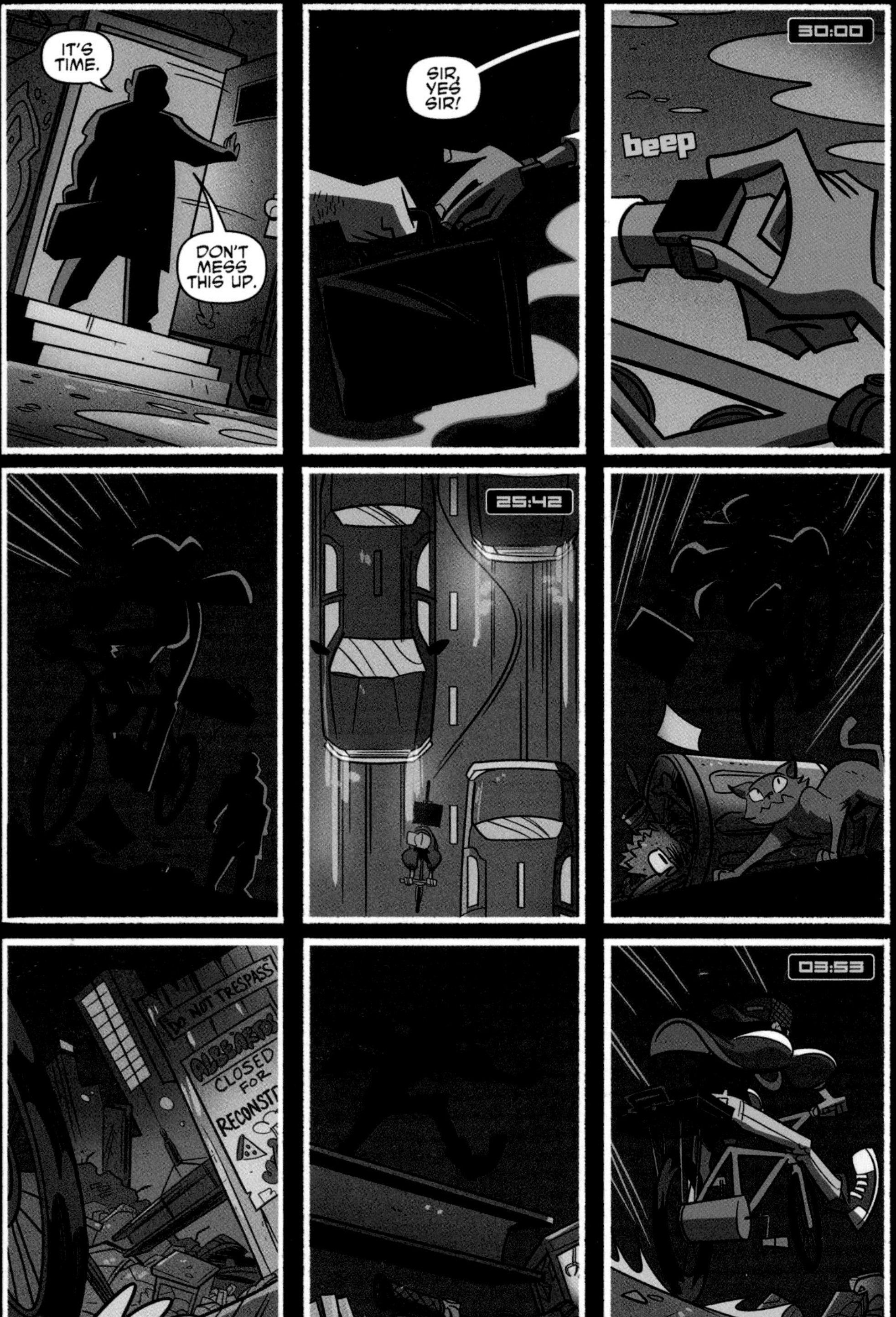
IT'S TIME.
DON'T MESS THIS UP.
SIR, YES SIR!
30:00
beep
25:42
DO NOT TRESPASS
CLOSED FOR
12:27
03:53

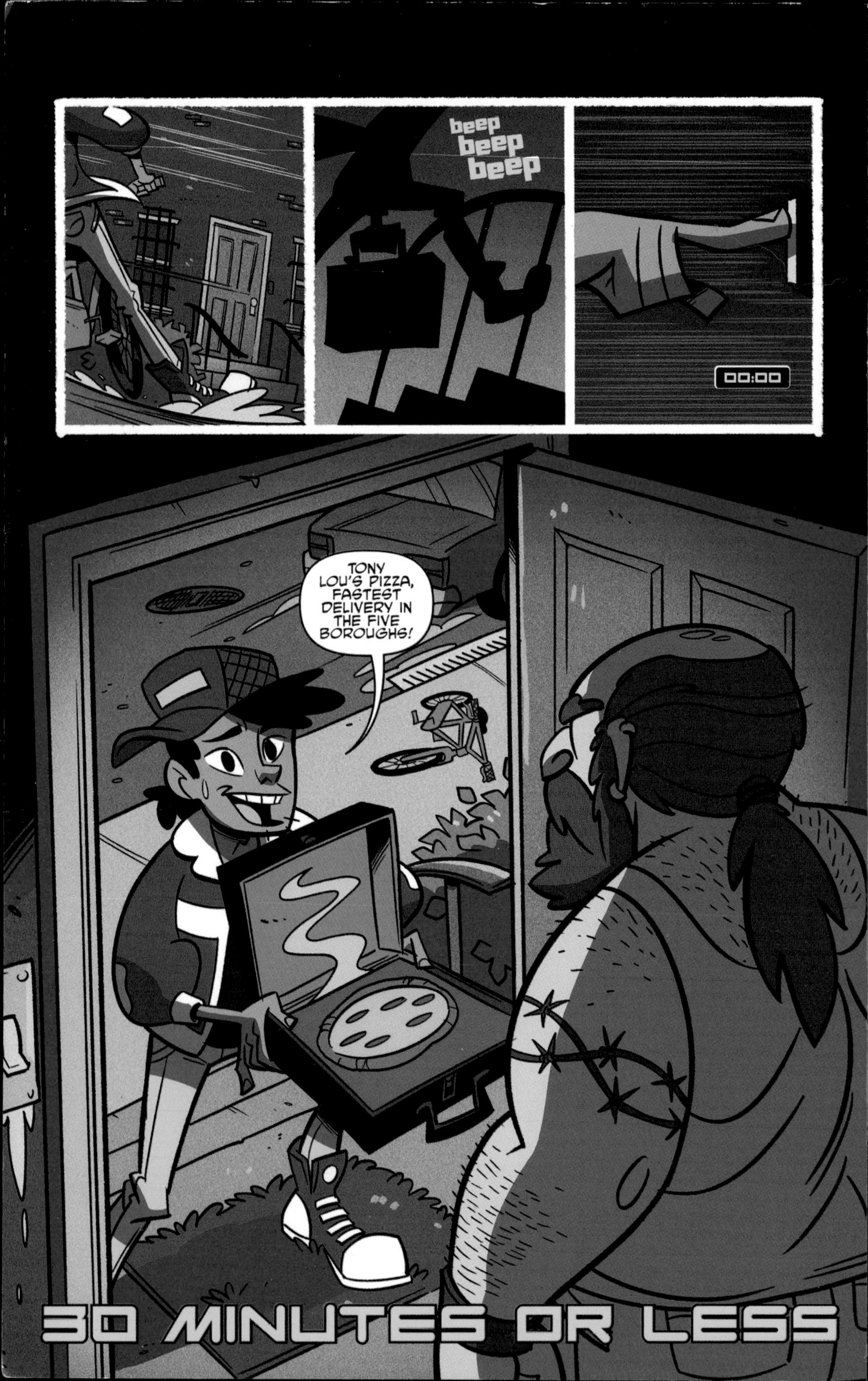
beep
beep
beep
00:00
TONY LOU'S PIZZA, FASTEST DELIVERY IN THE FIVE BOROUGHS!
30 MINUTES OR LESS

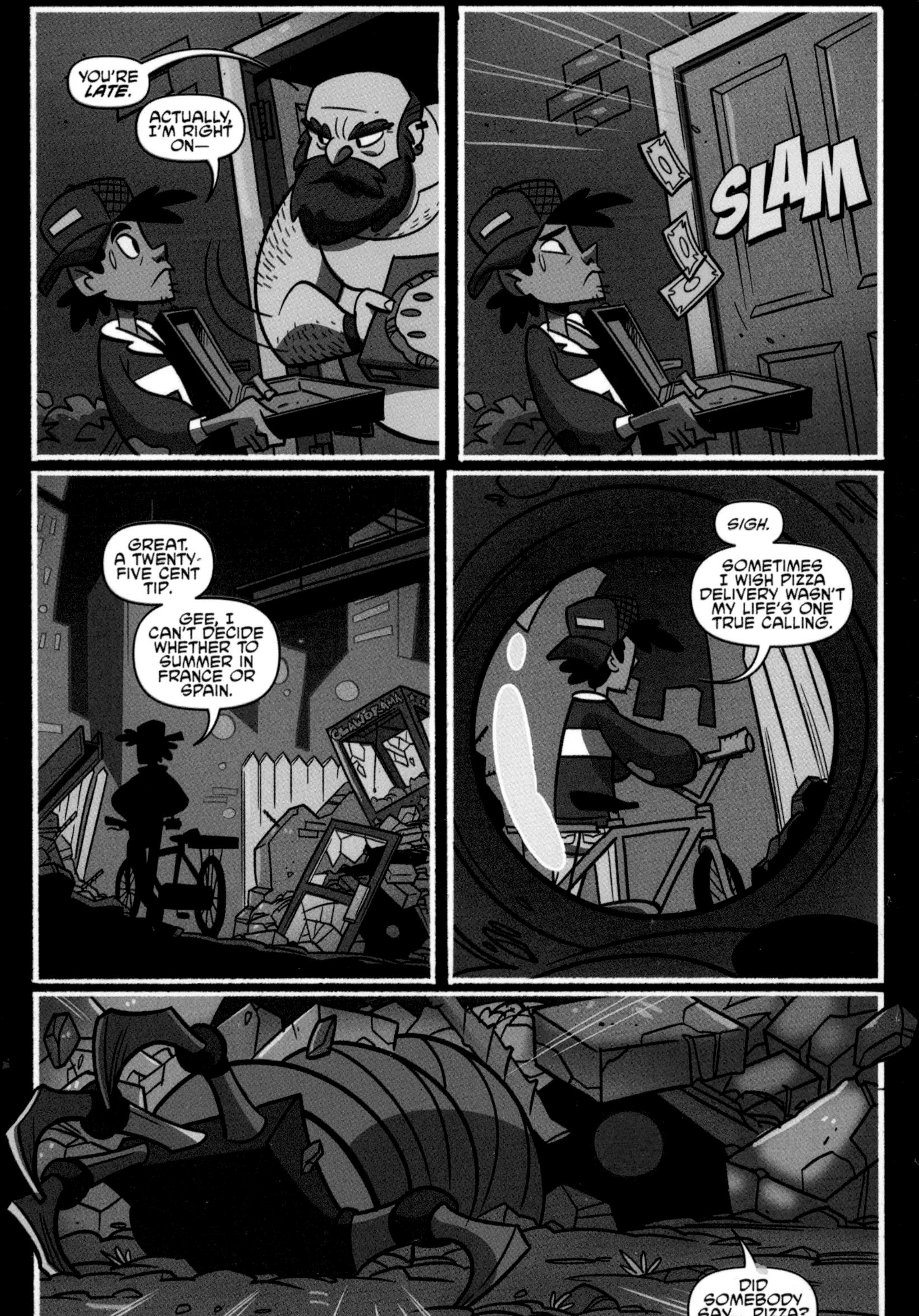

YOU'RE LATE.
ACTUALLY, I'M RIGHT ON—
SLAM
GREAT. A TWENTY-FIVE CENT TIP.
GEE, I CAN'T DECIDE WHETHER TO SUMMER IN FRANCE OR SPAIN.
CLAWDRAMA
SIGH.
SOMETIMES I WISH PIZZA DELIVERY WASN'T MY LIFE'S ONE TRUE CALLING.
DID SOMEBODY SAY... PIZZA?

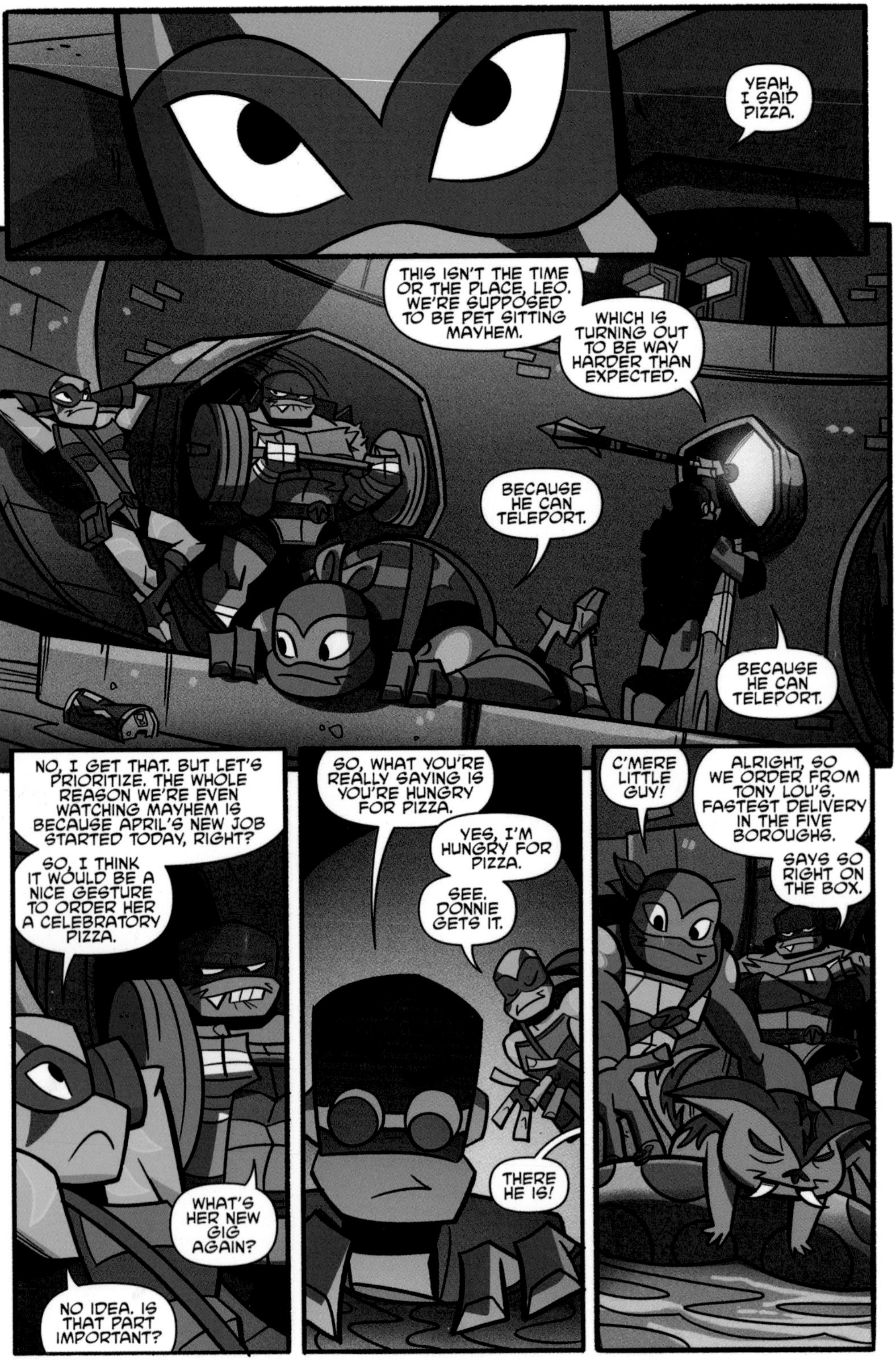
YEAH, I SAID PIZZA.
THIS ISN'T THE TIME OR THE PLACE, LEO. WE'RE SUPPOSED TO BE PET SITTING MAYHEM.
WHICH IS TURNING OUT TO BE WAY HARDER THAN EXPECTED.
BECAUSE HE CAN TELEPORT.
BECAUSE HE CAN TELEPORT.
NO, I GET THAT. BUT LET'S PRIORITIZE. THE WHOLE REASON WE'RE EVEN WATCHING MAYHEM IS BECAUSE APRIL'S NEW JOB STARTED TODAY, RIGHT?
SO, I THINK IT WOULD BE A NICE GESTURE TO ORDER HER A CELEBRATORY PIZZA.
WHAT'S HER NEW GIG AGAIN?
NO IDEA. IS THAT PART IMPORTANT?
SO, WHAT YOU'RE REALLY SAYING IS YOU'RE HUNGRY FOR PIZZA.
YES, I'M HUNGRY FOR PIZZA.
SEE. DONNIE GETS IT.
THERE HE IS!
C'MERE LITTLE GUY!
ALRIGHT, SO WE ORDER FROM TONY LOU'S. FASTEST DELIVERY IN THE FIVE BOROUGHS.
SAYS SO RIGHT ON THE BOX.

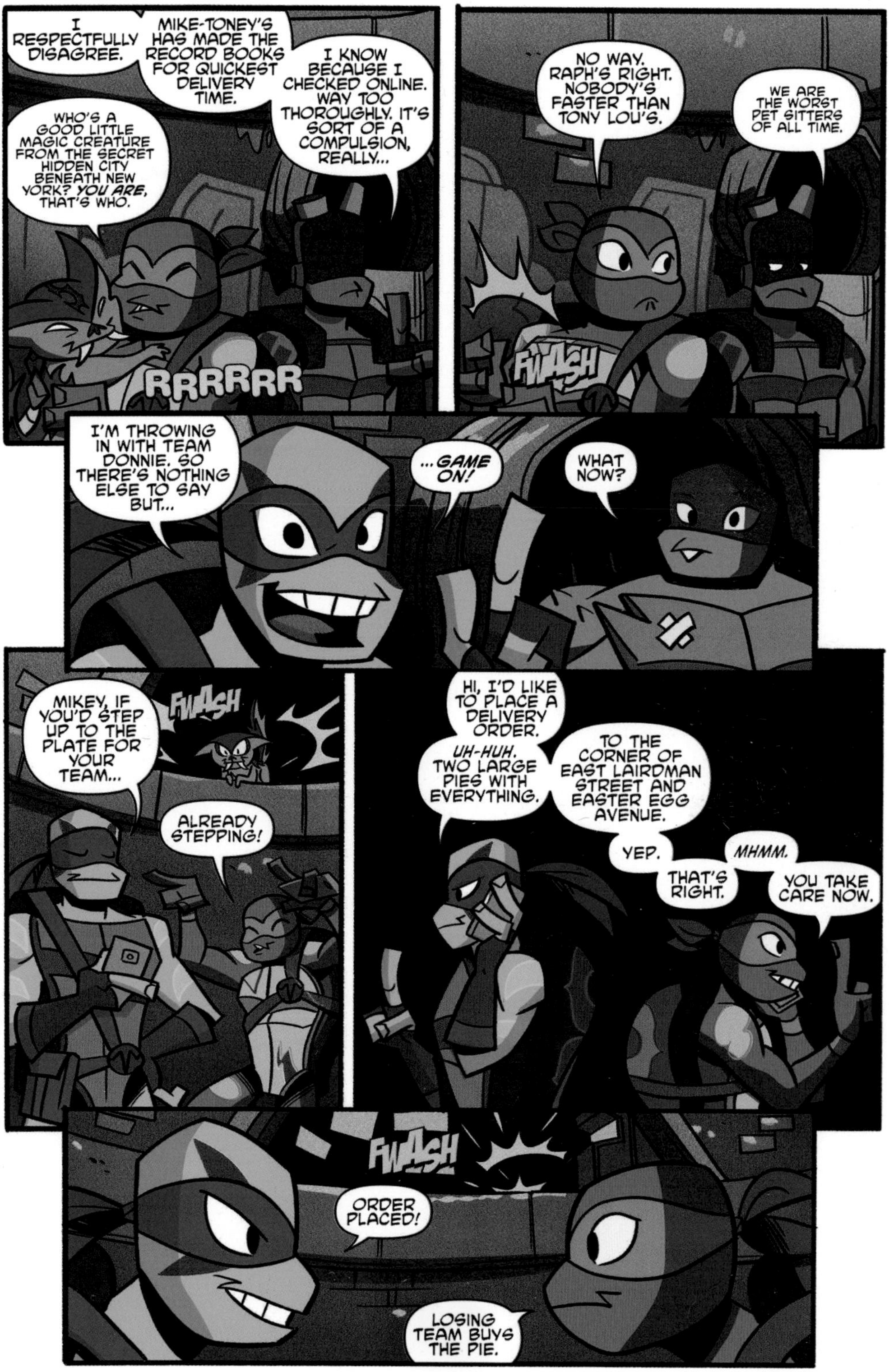
I RESPECTFULLY DISAGREE.
MIKE-TONEY'S HAS MADE THE RECORD BOOKS FOR QUICKEST DELIVERY TIME.
I KNOW BECAUSE I CHECKED ONLINE. WAY TOO THOROUGHLY. IT'S SORT OF A COMPULSION, REALLY...
WHO'S A GOOD LITTLE MAGIC CREATURE FROM THE SECRET HIDDEN CITY BENEATH NEW YORK? *YOU ARE,* THAT'S WHO.
RRRRRR
NO WAY. RAPH'S RIGHT. NOBODY'S FASTER THAN TONY LOU'S.
WE ARE THE WORST PET SITTERS OF ALL TIME.
FWASH
I'M THROWING IN WITH TEAM DONNIE. SO THERE'S NOTHING ELSE TO SAY BUT...
...GAME ON!
WHAT NOW?
MIKEY, IF YOU'D STEP UP TO THE PLATE FOR YOUR TEAM...
FWASH
ALREADY STEPPING!
HI, I'D LIKE TO PLACE A DELIVERY ORDER.
UH-HUH. TWO LARGE PIES WITH EVERYTHING.
TO THE CORNER OF EAST LAIRDMAN STREET AND EASTER EGG AVENUE.
YEP.
THAT'S RIGHT.
MHMM.
YOU TAKE CARE NOW.
FWASH
ORDER PLACED!
LOSING TEAM BUYS THE PIE.

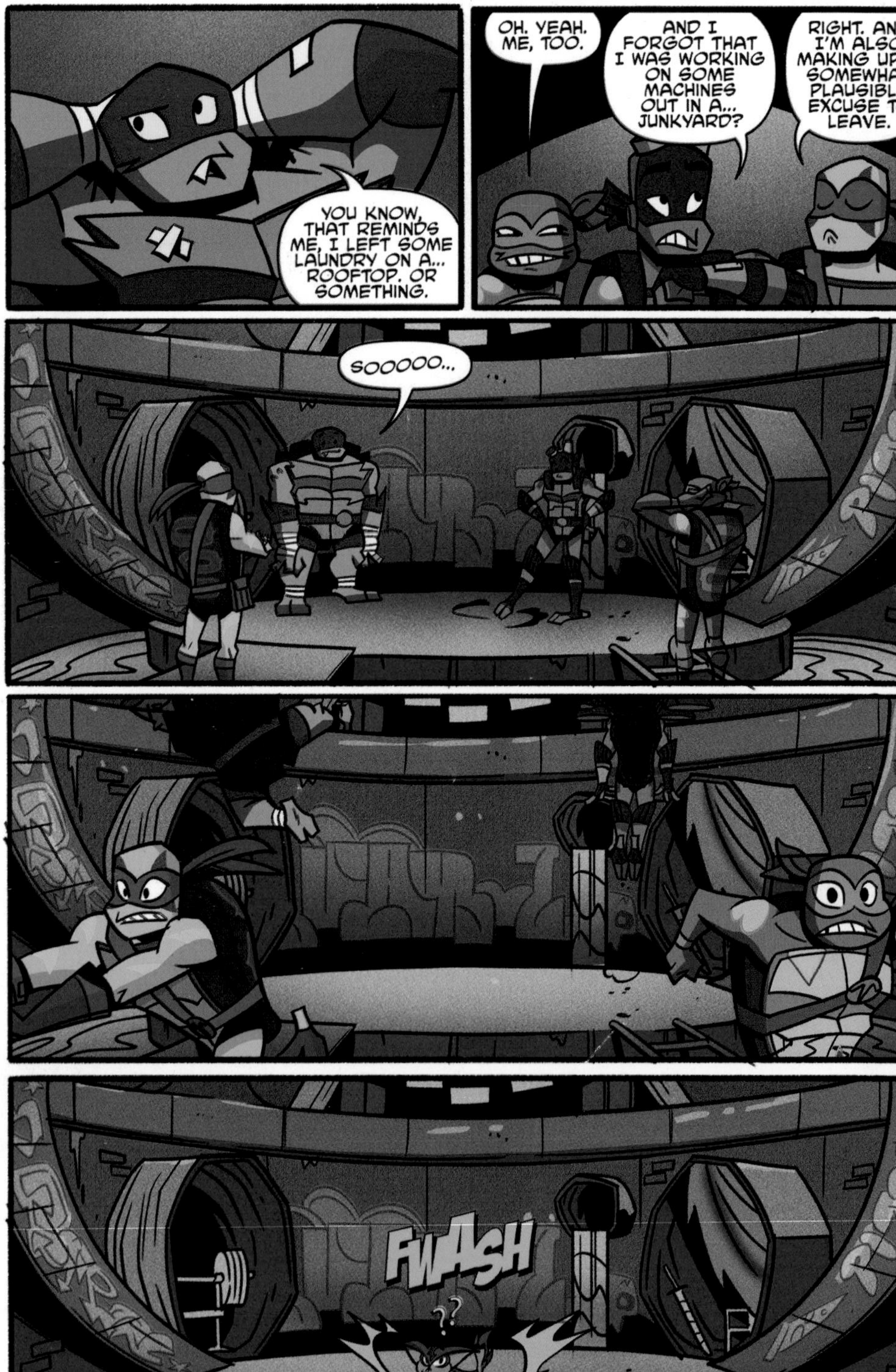
YOU KNOW, THAT REMINDS ME, I LEFT SOME LAUNDRY ON A... ROOFTOP. OR SOMETHING.
OH. YEAH. ME, TOO.
AND I FORGOT THAT I WAS WORKING ON SOME MACHINES OUT IN A... JUNKYARD?
RIGHT. AND I'M ALSO MAKING UP A SOMEWHAT PLAUSIBLE EXCUSE TO LEAVE.
SOOOOO...
FWASH
??

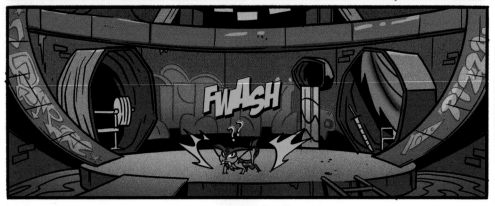

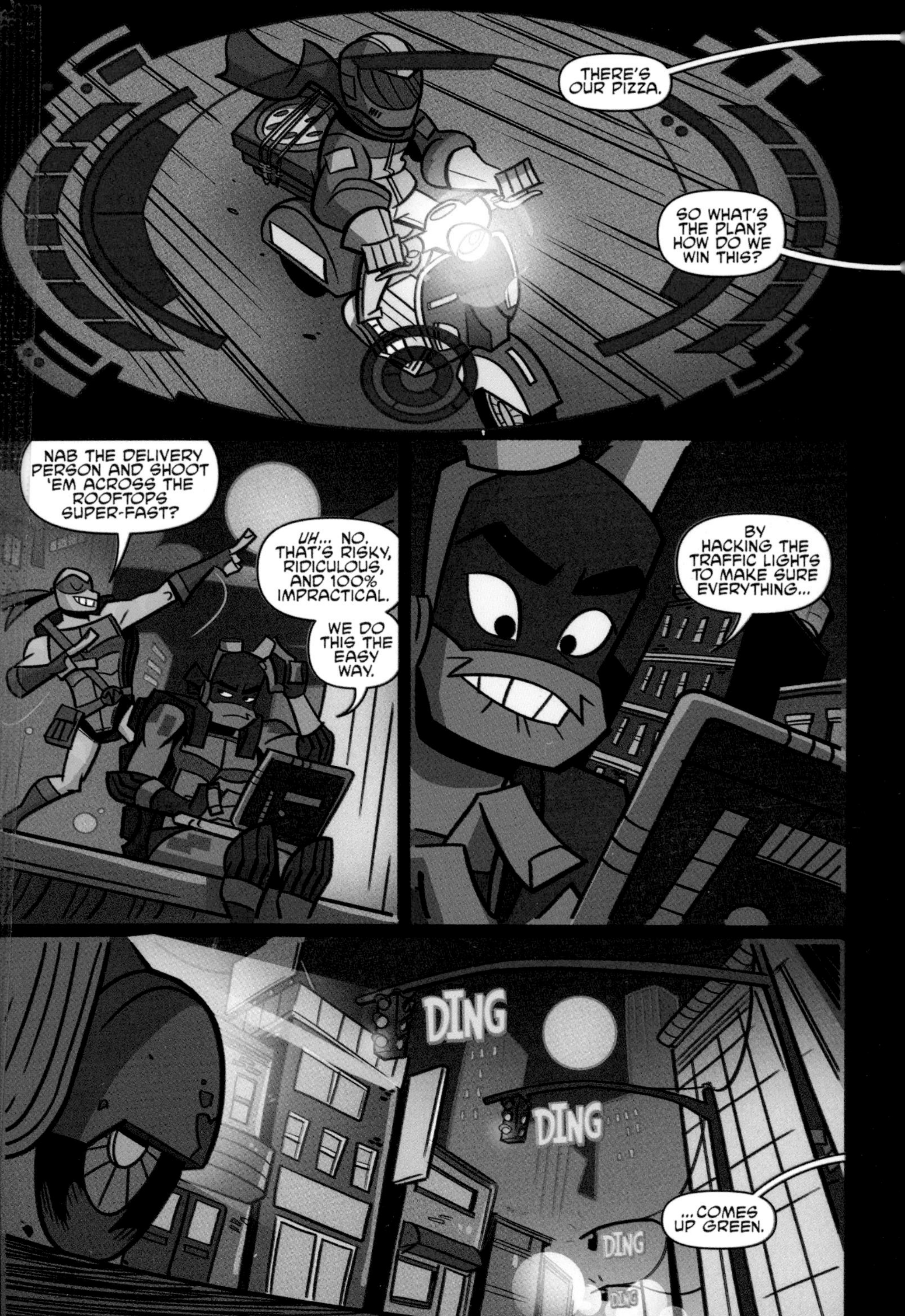
THERE'S OUR PIZZA.
SO WHAT'S THE PLAN? HOW DO WE WIN THIS?
NAB THE DELIVERY PERSON AND SHOOT 'EM ACROSS THE ROOFTOPS SUPER-FAST?
UH... NO. THAT'S RISKY, RIDICULOUS, AND 100% IMPRACTICAL.
WE DO THIS THE EASY WAY.
BY HACKING THE TRAFFIC LIGHTS TO MAKE SURE EVERYTHING...
DING
DING
...COMES UP GREEN.
DING
DING

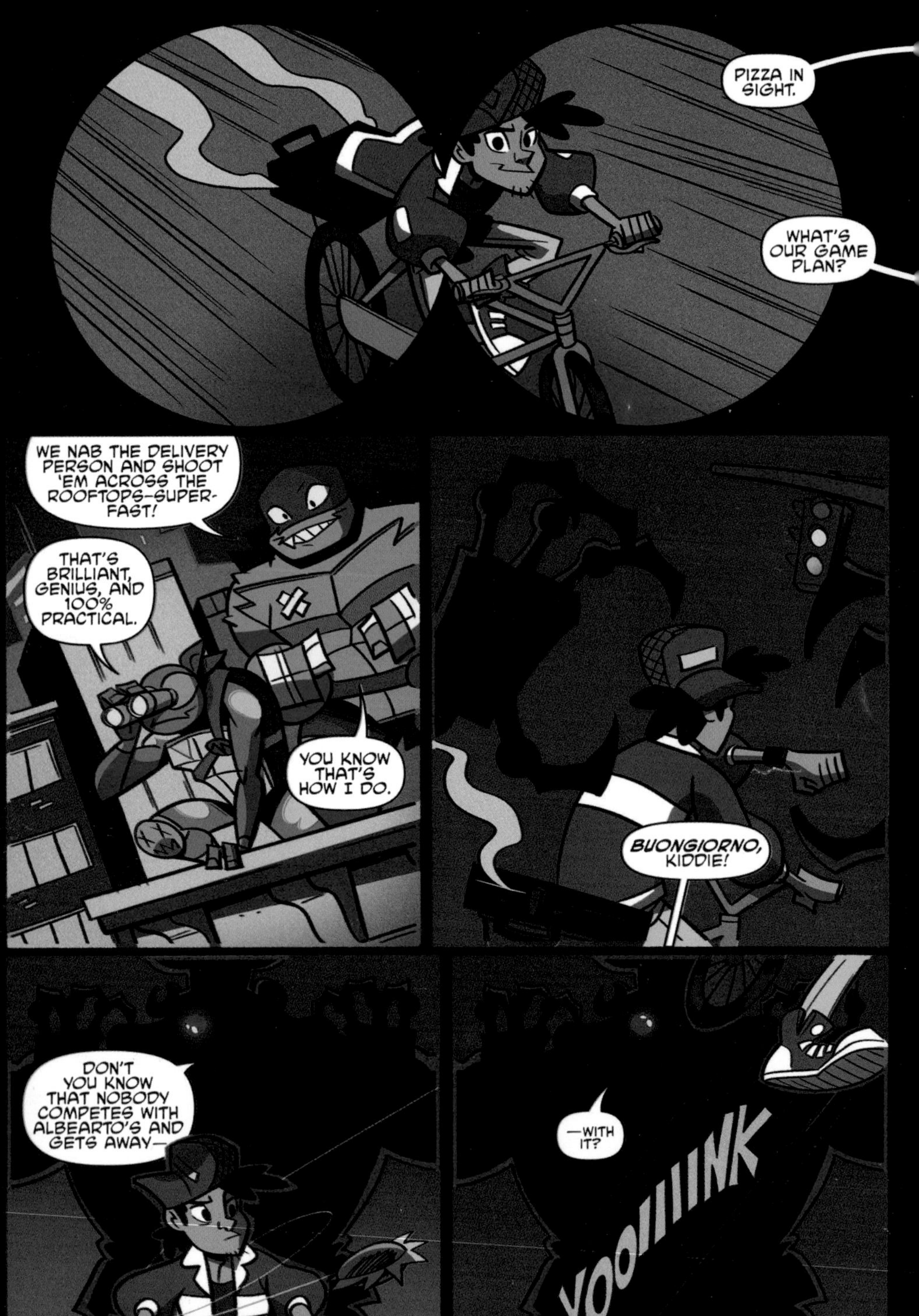

PIZZA IN SIGHT.
WHAT'S OUR GAME PLAN?
WE NAB THE DELIVERY PERSON AND SHOOT 'EM ACROSS THE ROOFTOPS—SUPER-FAST!
THAT'S BRILLIANT, GENIUS, AND 100% PRACTICAL.
YOU KNOW THAT'S HOW I DO.
BUONGIORNO, KIDDIE!
DON'T YOU KNOW THAT NOBODY COMPETES WITH ALBEARTO'S AND GETS AWAY—
—WITH IT?
YOOIIIIINK

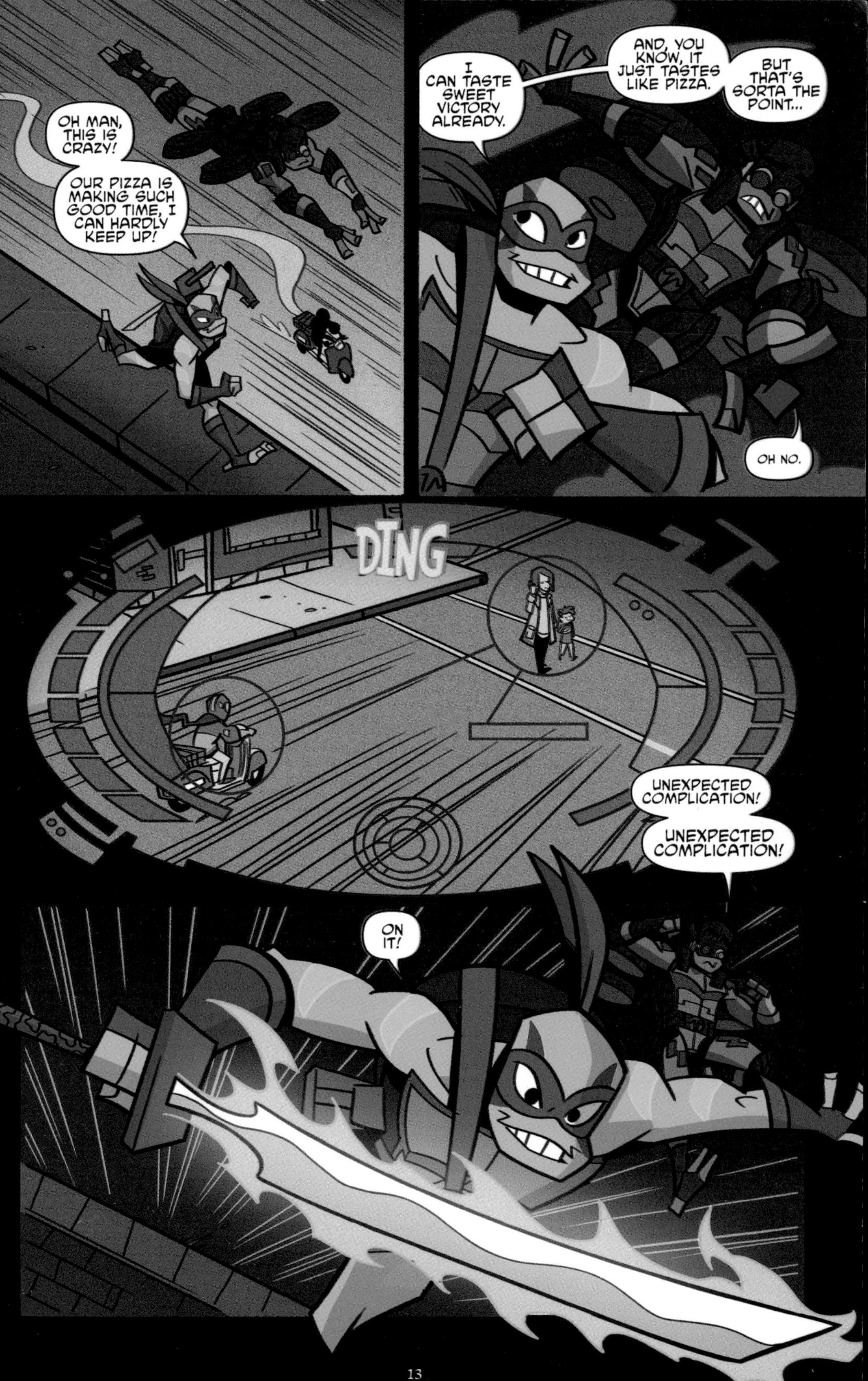
OH MAN, THIS IS CRAZY!
OUR PIZZA IS MAKING SUCH GOOD TIME, I CAN HARDLY KEEP UP!
I CAN TASTE SWEET VICTORY ALREADY.
AND, YOU KNOW, IT JUST TASTES LIKE PIZZA.
BUT THAT'S SORTA THE POINT...
OH NO.
DING
UNEXPECTED COMPLICATION!
UNEXPECTED COMPLICATION!
ON IT!

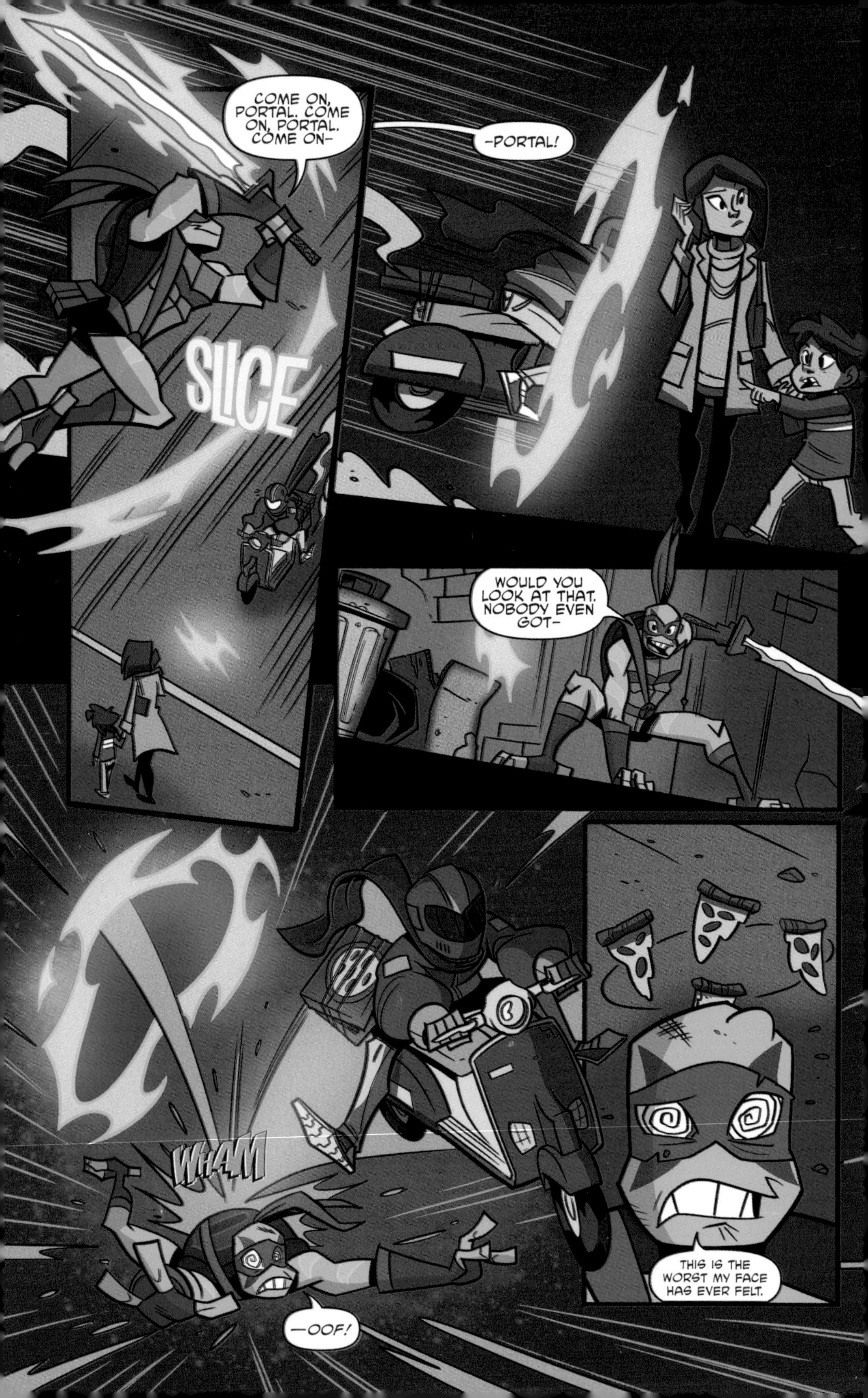
COME ON, PORTAL. COME ON, PORTAL. COME ON-
-PORTAL!
SLICE
WOULD YOU LOOK AT THAT. NOBODY EVEN GOT-
WHAM
—OOF!
THIS IS THE WORST MY FACE HAS EVER FELT.

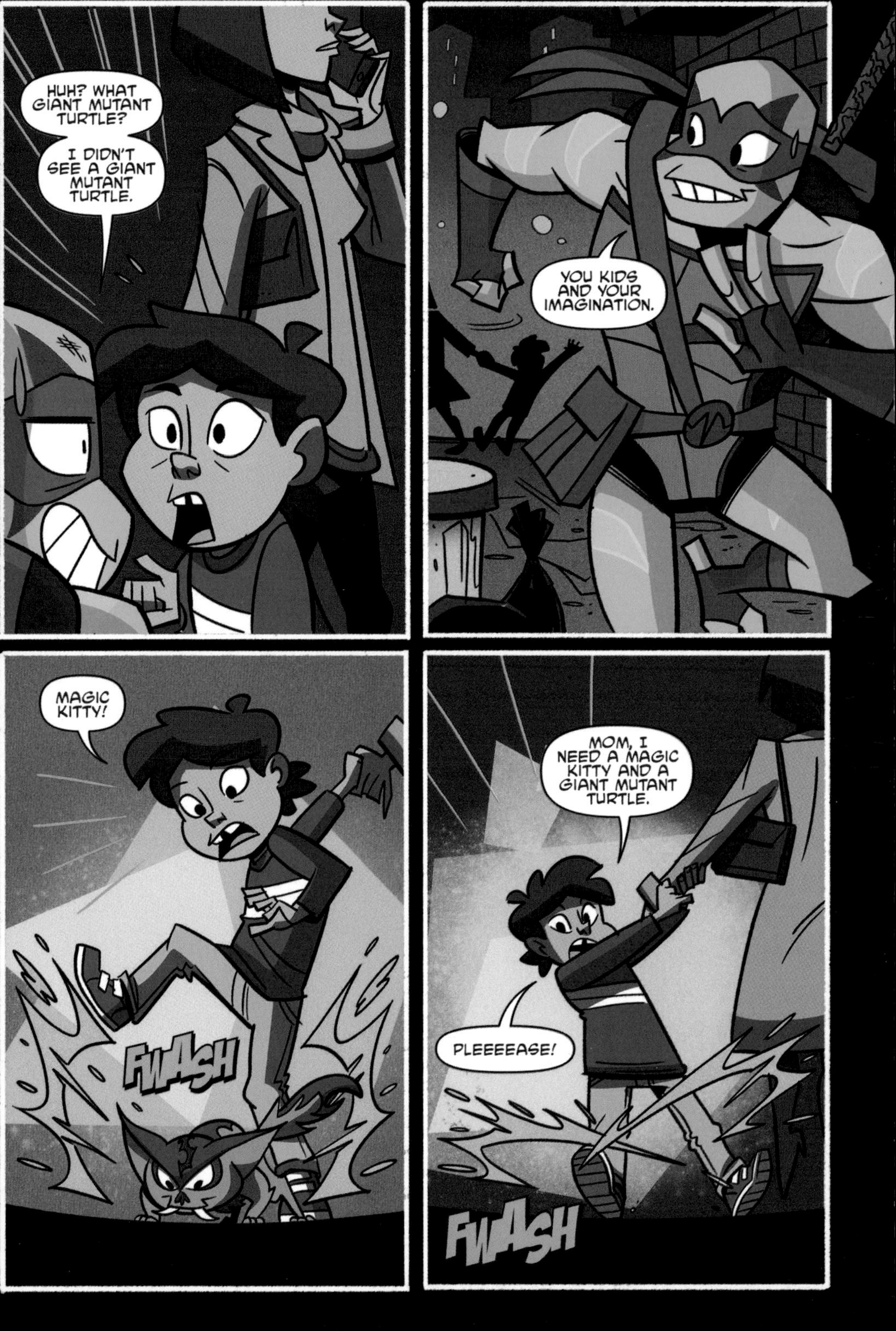
HUH? WHAT GIANT MUTANT TURTLE?
I DIDN'T SEE A GIANT MUTANT TURTLE.
YOU KIDS AND YOUR IMAGINATION.
MAGIC KITTY!
FWASH
MOM, I NEED A MAGIC KITTY AND A GIANT MUTANT TURTLE.
PLEEEEEASE!
FWASH

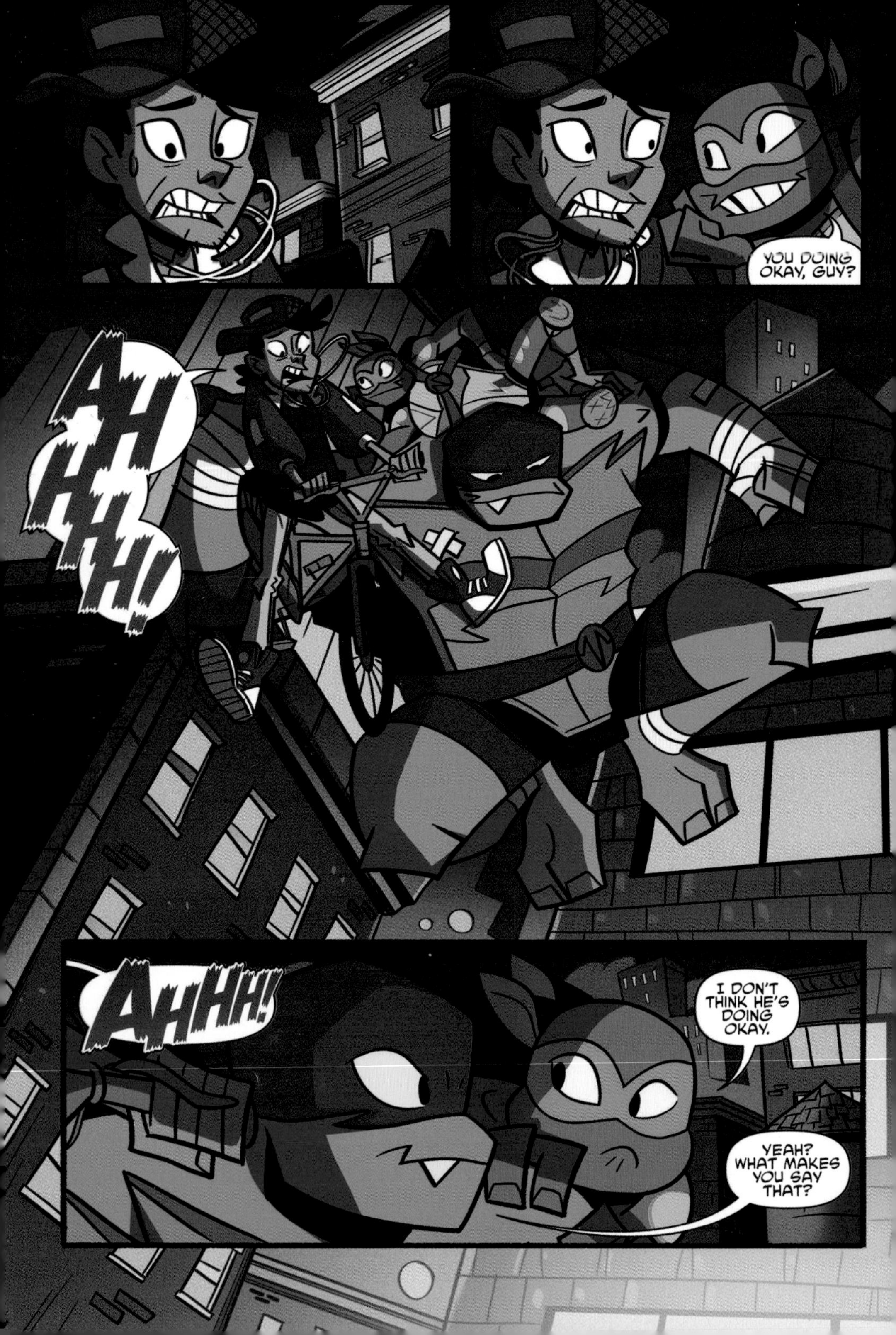
YOU DOING OKAY, GUY?
AHHHH!
AHHH!
I DON'T THINK HE'S DOING OKAY.
YEAH? WHAT MAKES YOU SAY THAT?

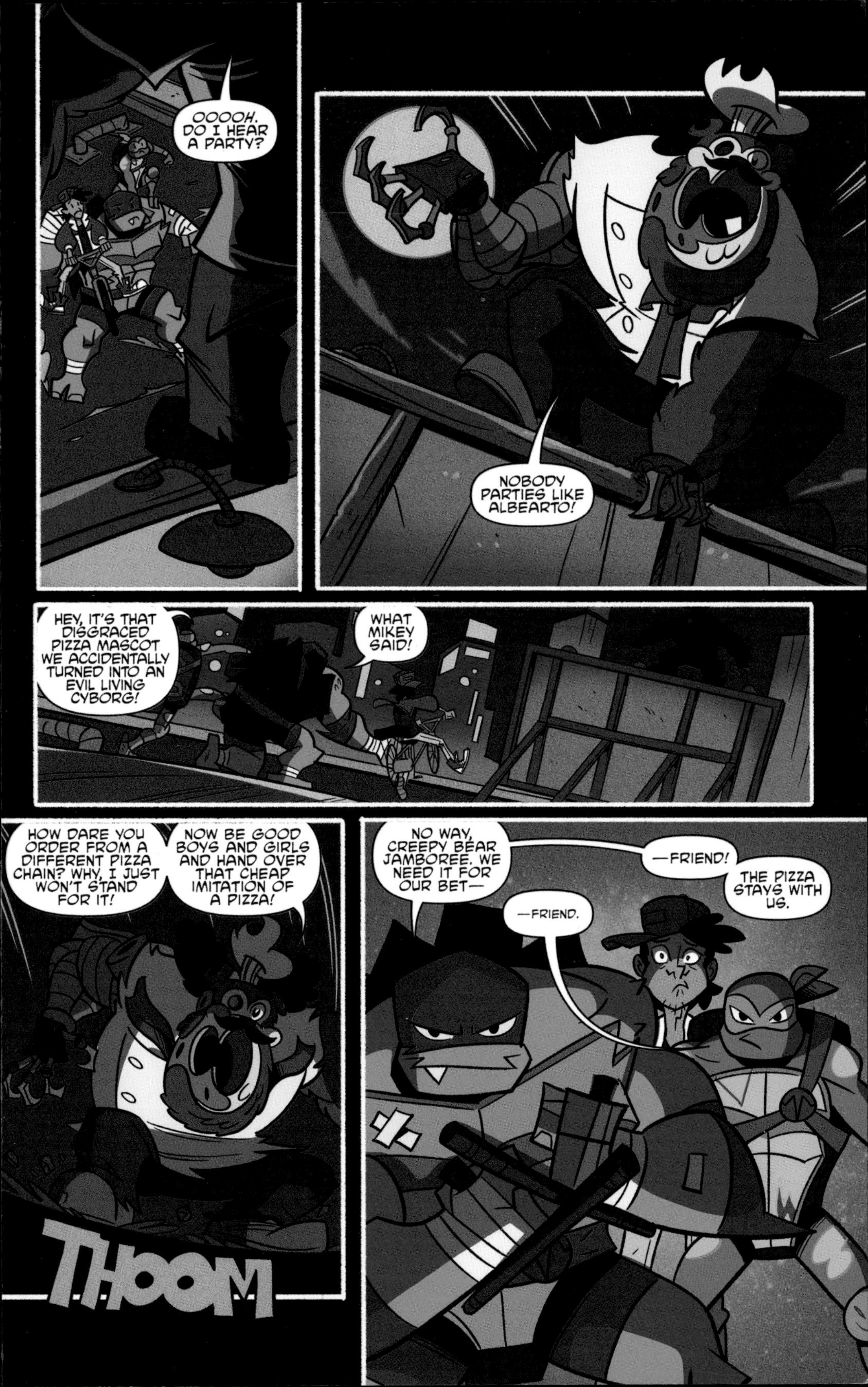
OOOOH. DO I HEAR A PARTY?
NOBODY PARTIES LIKE ALBEARTO!
HEY, IT'S THAT DISGRACED PIZZA MASCOT WE ACCIDENTALLY TURNED INTO AN EVIL LIVING CYBORG!
WHAT MIKEY SAID!
HOW DARE YOU ORDER FROM A DIFFERENT PIZZA CHAIN? WHY, I JUST WON'T STAND FOR IT!
NOW BE GOOD BOYS AND GIRLS AND HAND OVER THAT CHEAP IMITATION OF A PIZZA!
THOOM
NO WAY, CREEPY BEAR JAMBOREE. WE NEED IT FOR OUR BET—
—FRIEND.
—FRIEND!
THE PIZZA STAYS WITH US.

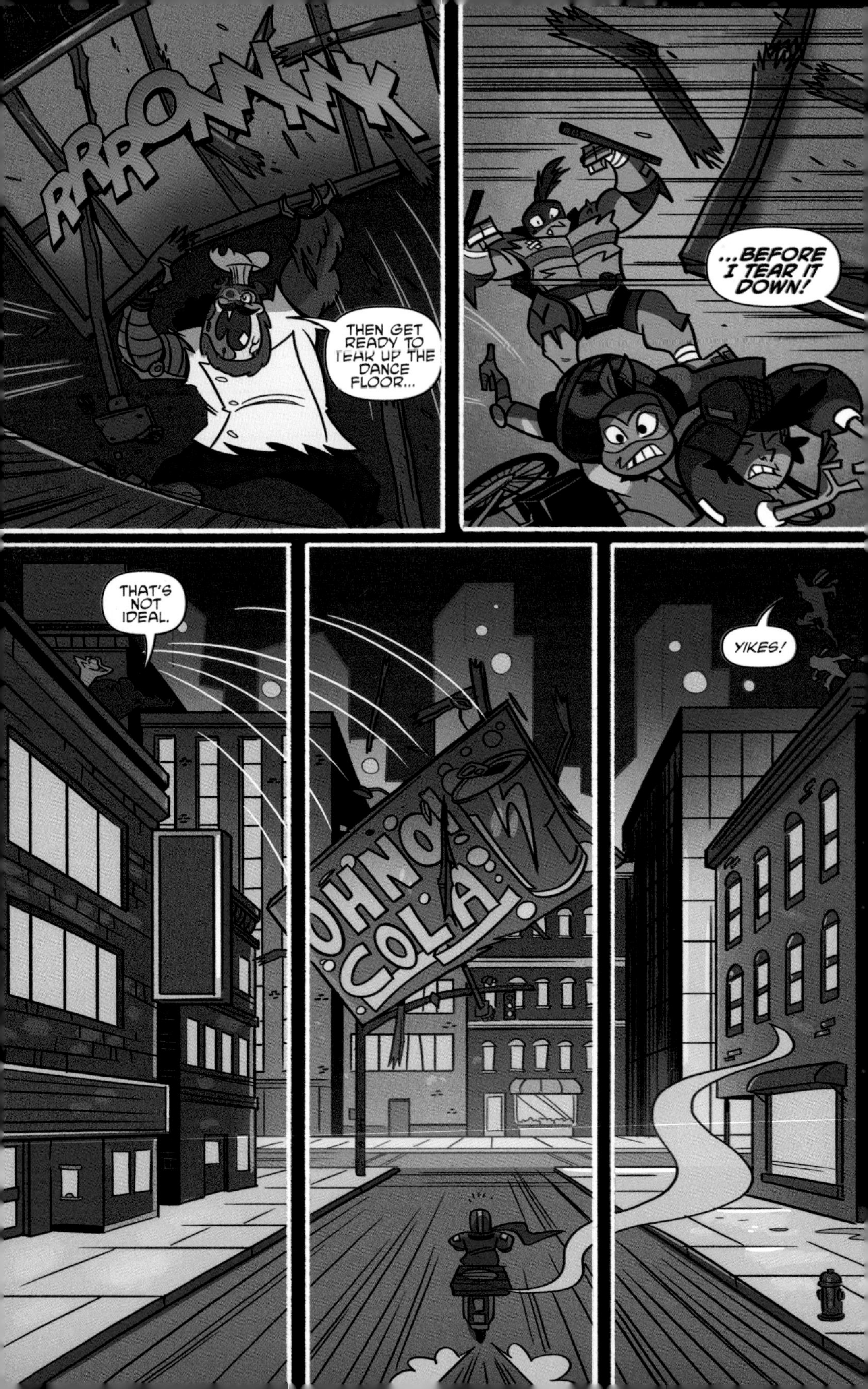
RRRONNNK
THEN GET READY TO TEAR UP THE DANCE FLOOR...
...BEFORE I TEAR IT DOWN!
THAT'S NOT IDEAL.
OHNO COLA
YIKES!

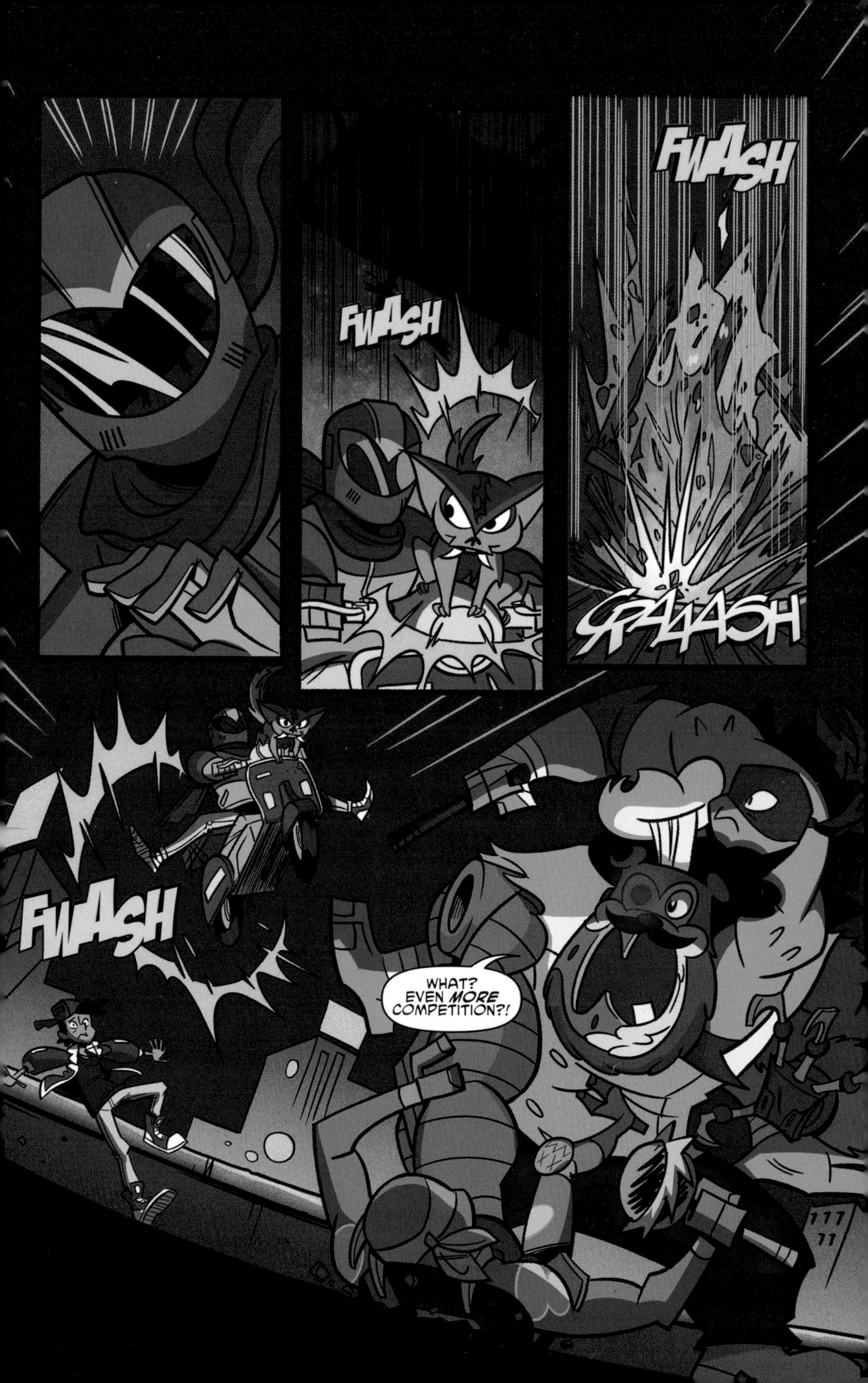
FWASH
FWASH
CRAAASH
FWASH
WHAT? EVEN MORE COMPETITION?!

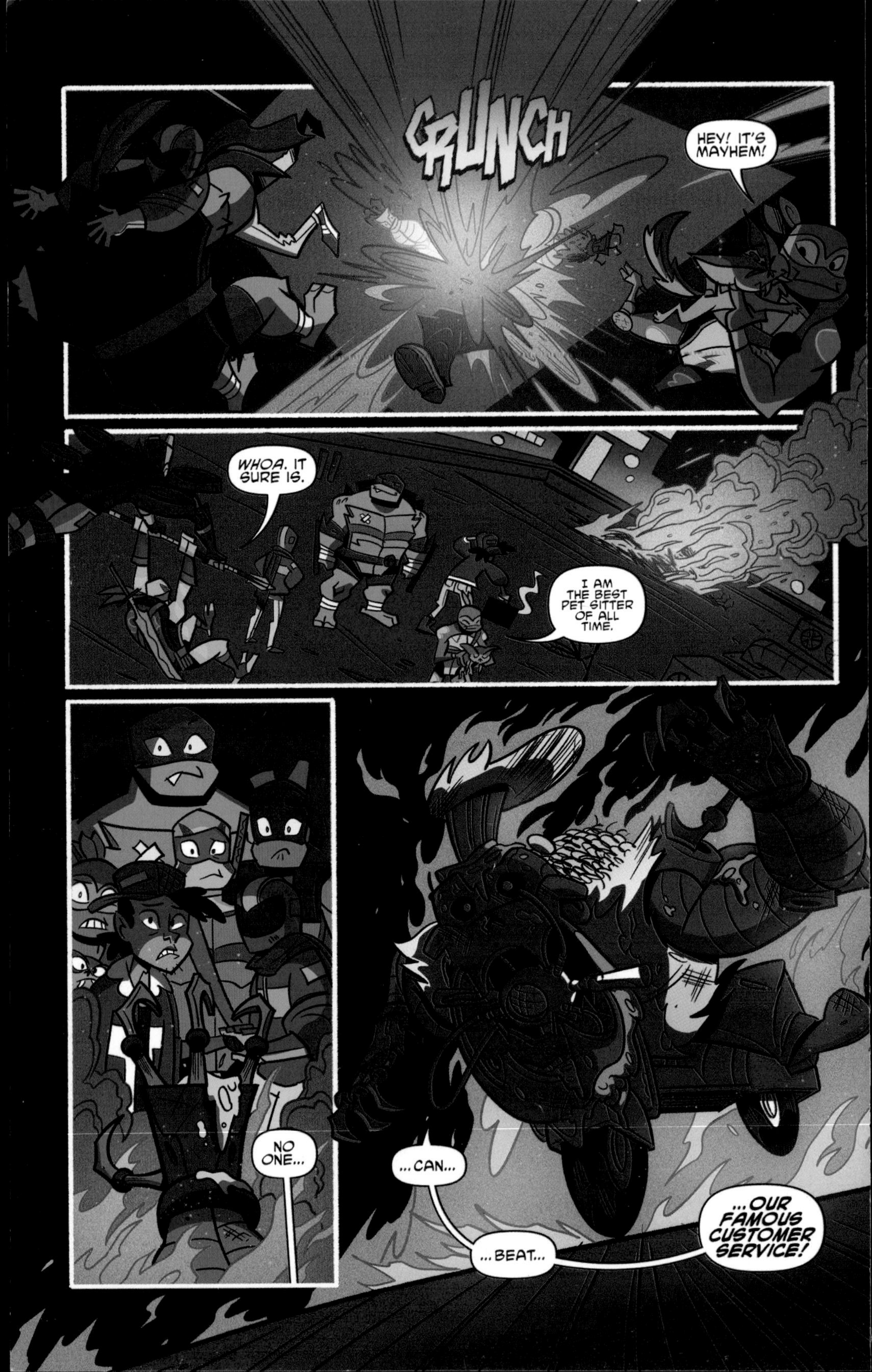
CRUNCH
HEY! IT'S MAYHEM!
WHOA. IT SURE IS.
I AM THE BEST PET SITTER OF ALL TIME.
NO ONE...
...CAN...
...BEAT...
...OUR FAMOUS CUSTOMER SERVICE!

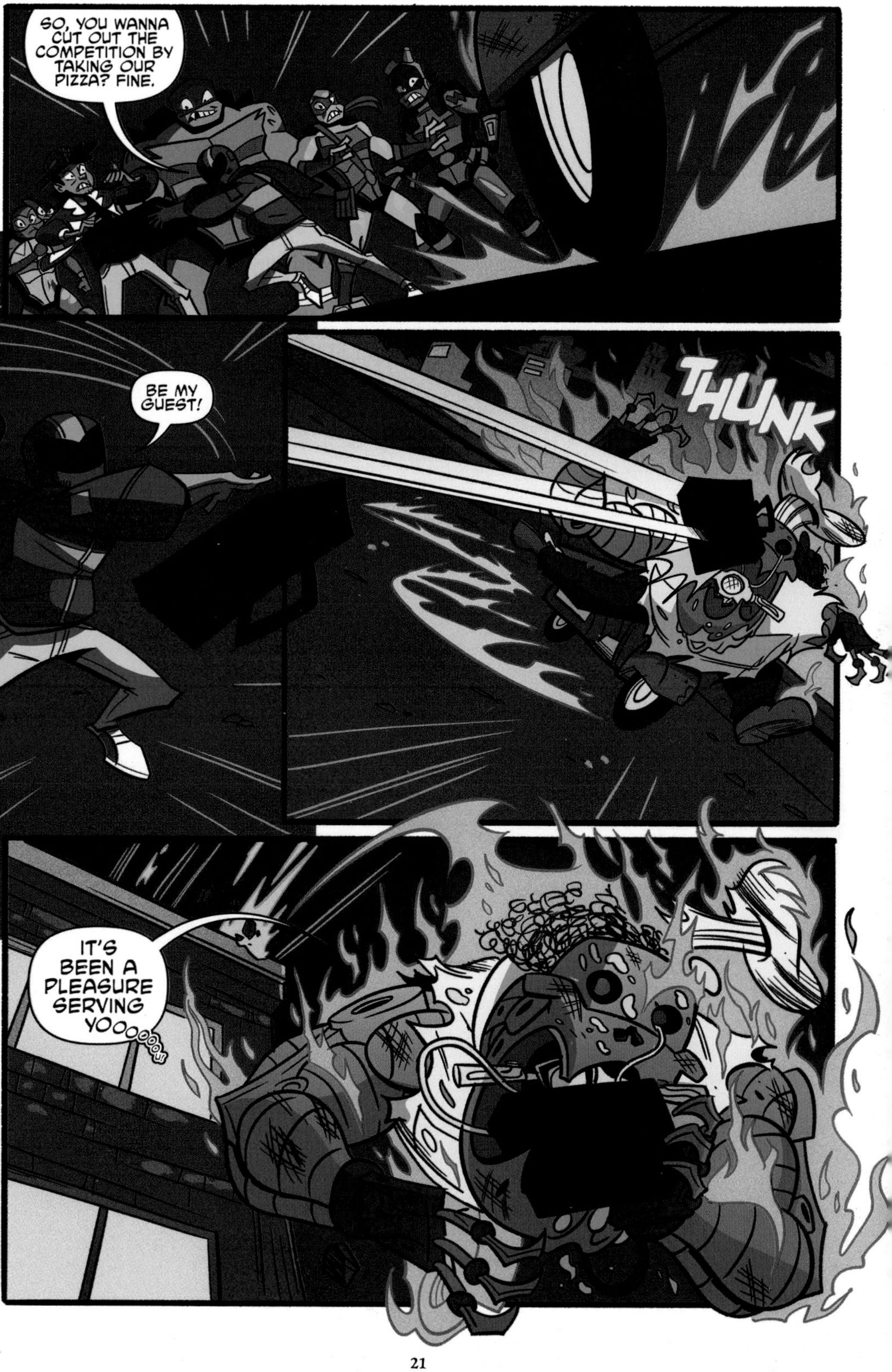

SO, YOU WANNA CUT OUT THE COMPETITION BY TAKING OUR PIZZA? FINE.
BE MY GUEST!
THUNK
IT'S BEEN A PLEASURE SERVING YOoooooo!

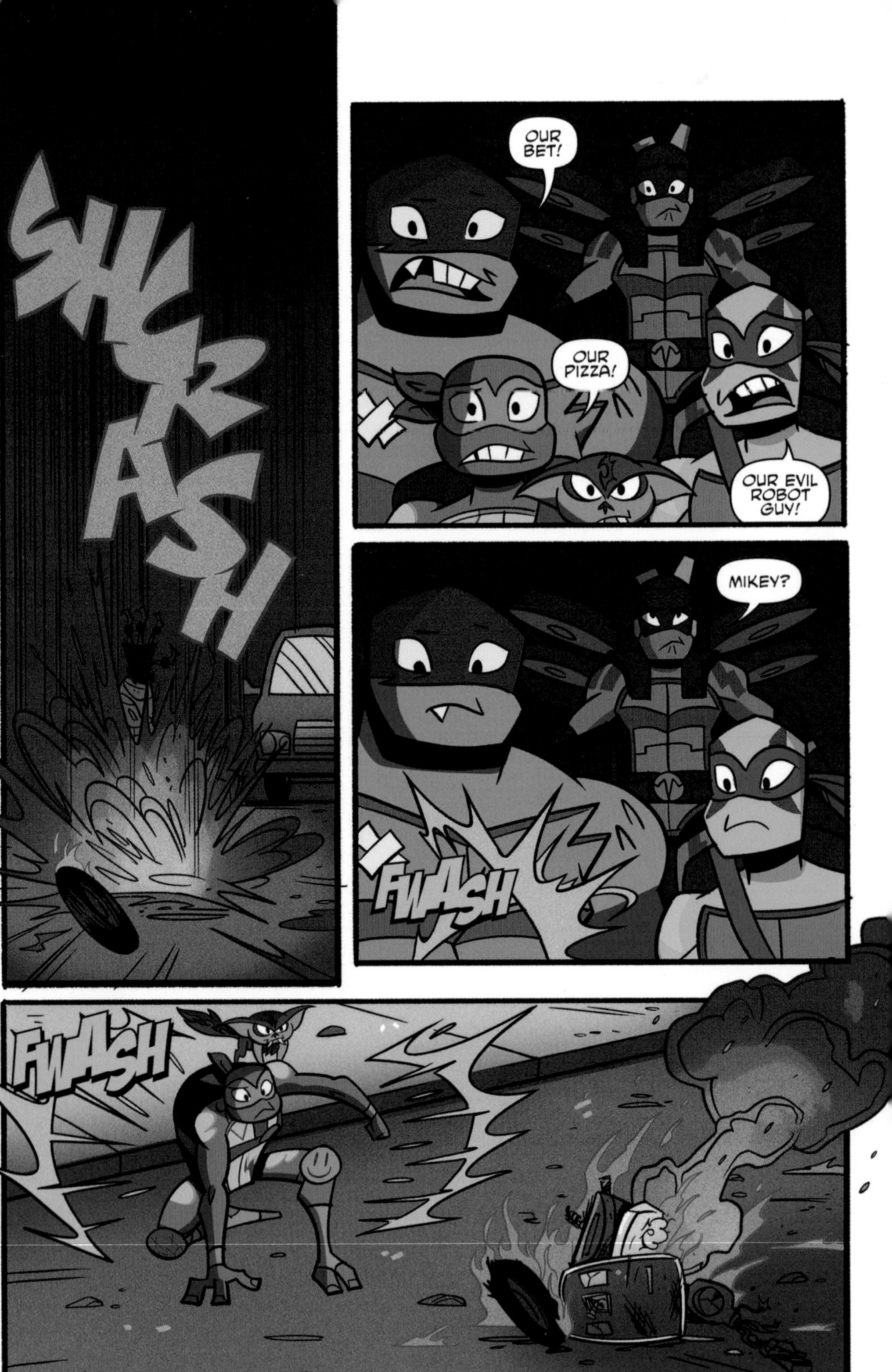
SHURASH
OUR BET!
OUR PIZZA!
OUR EVIL ROBOT GUY!
MIKEY?
FWASH
FWASH

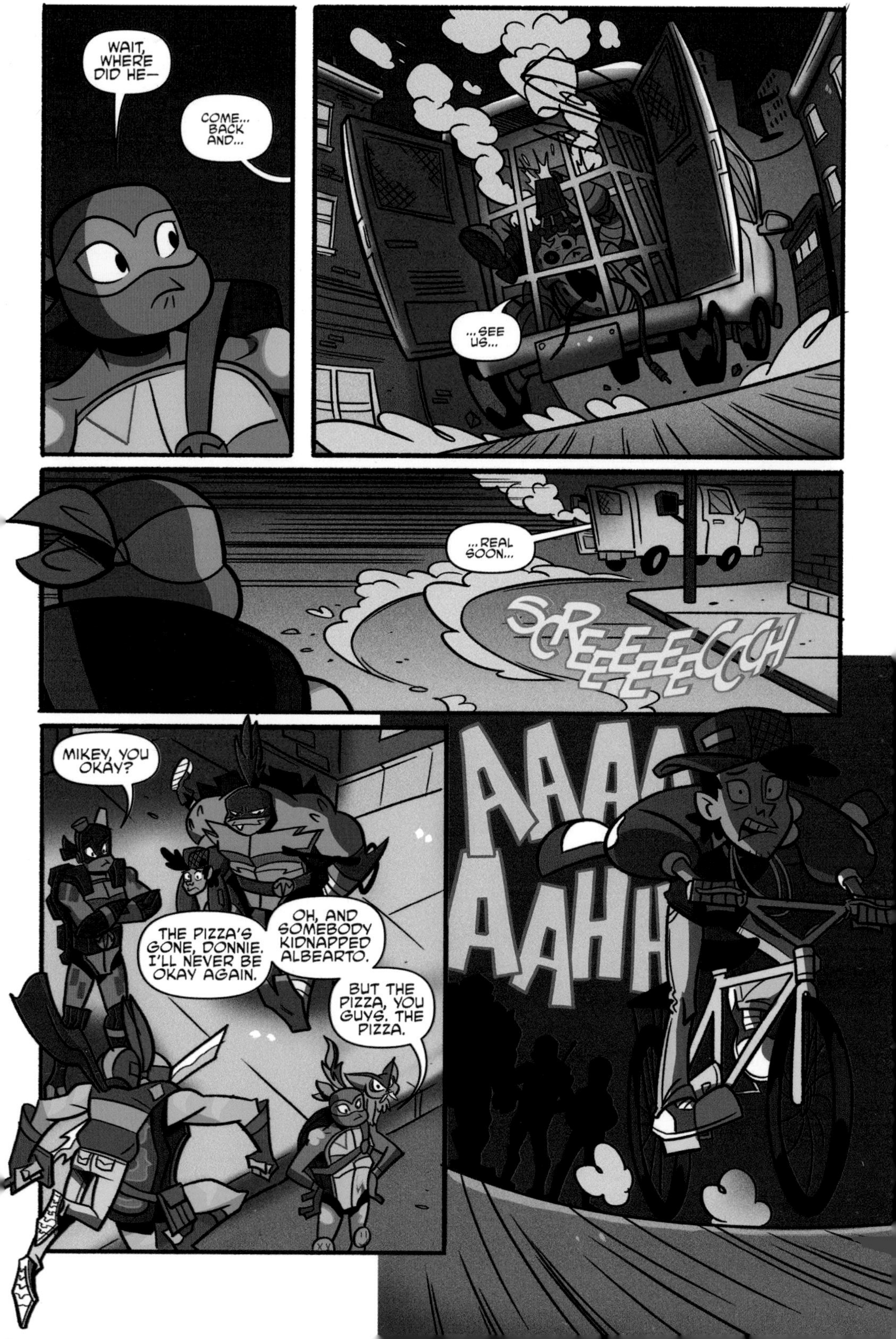
WAIT, WHERE DID HE—
COME... BACK AND...
...SEE US...
...REAL SOON...
SCREEEEEECCCH
MIKEY, YOU OKAY?
THE PIZZA'S GONE, DONNIE. I'LL NEVER BE OKAY AGAIN.
OH, AND SOMEBODY KIDNAPPED ALBEARTO.
BUT THE PIZZA, YOU GUYS. THE PIZZA.
AAAAAAHH

HUH. WHAT'S HIS DEAL?

PROBABLY FREAKED OUT BY ALL THE MUTANTS AND THE MULTIPLE NEAR-DEATH EXPERIENCES.

BUT I'M JUST SPITBALLING HERE.

APRIL?!

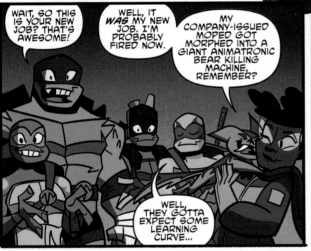

WAIT, SO THIS IS YOUR NEW JOB? THAT'S AWESOME!

WELL, IT *WAS* MY NEW JOB. I'M PROBABLY FIRED NOW.

MY COMPANY-ISSUED MOPED GOT MORPHED INTO A GIANT ANIMATRONIC BEAR KILLING MACHINE, REMEMBER?

WELL, THEY GOTTA EXPECT SOME LEARNING CURVE...

SO, WE NEVER DID FIGURE OUT WHO WON THAT BET.

NO, WE DIDN'T, DID WE?

RING RING RING

YEAH, YOU'RE GONNA WANNA GET THAT...

RING RING RING

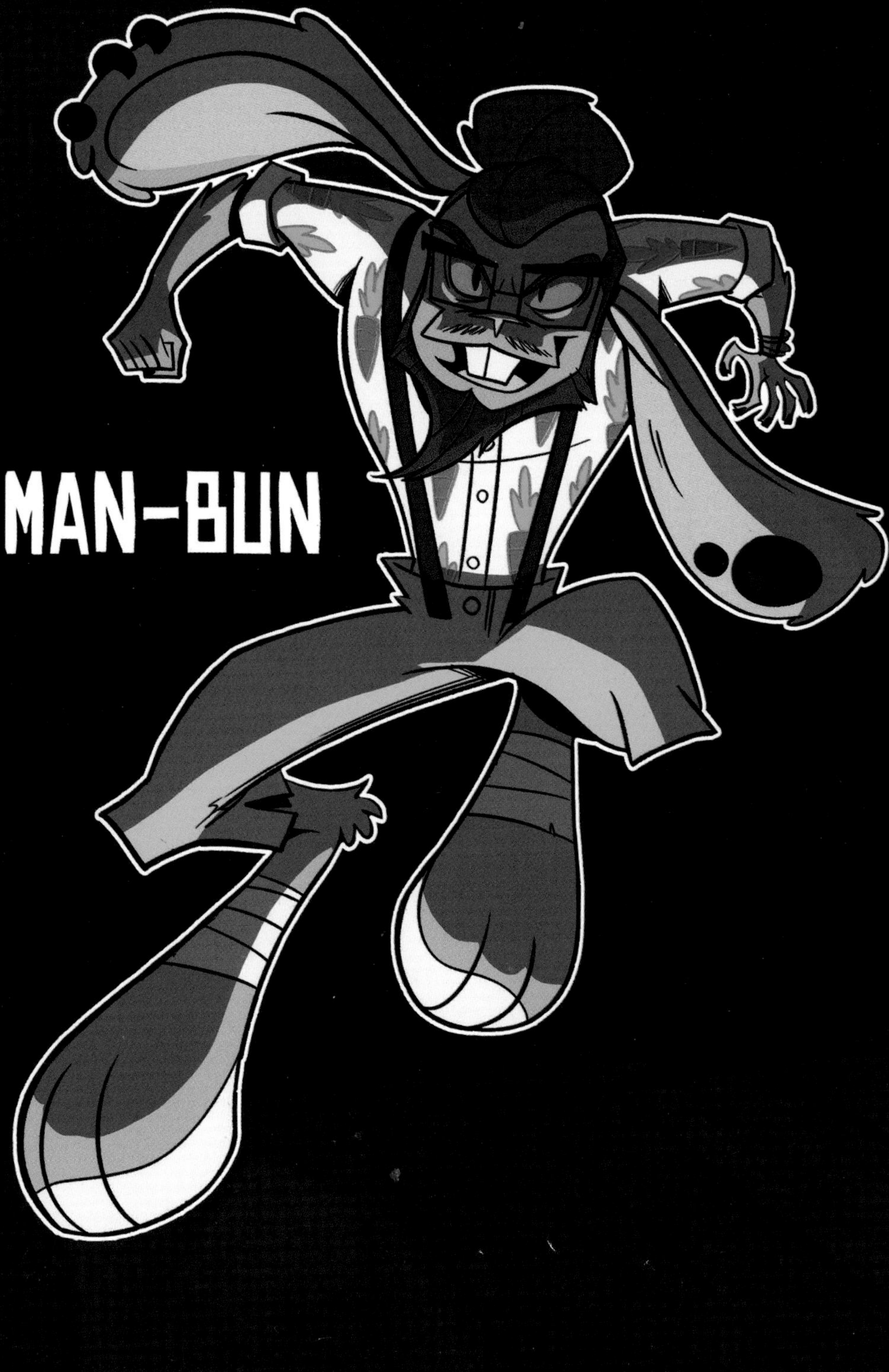
MAN-BUN

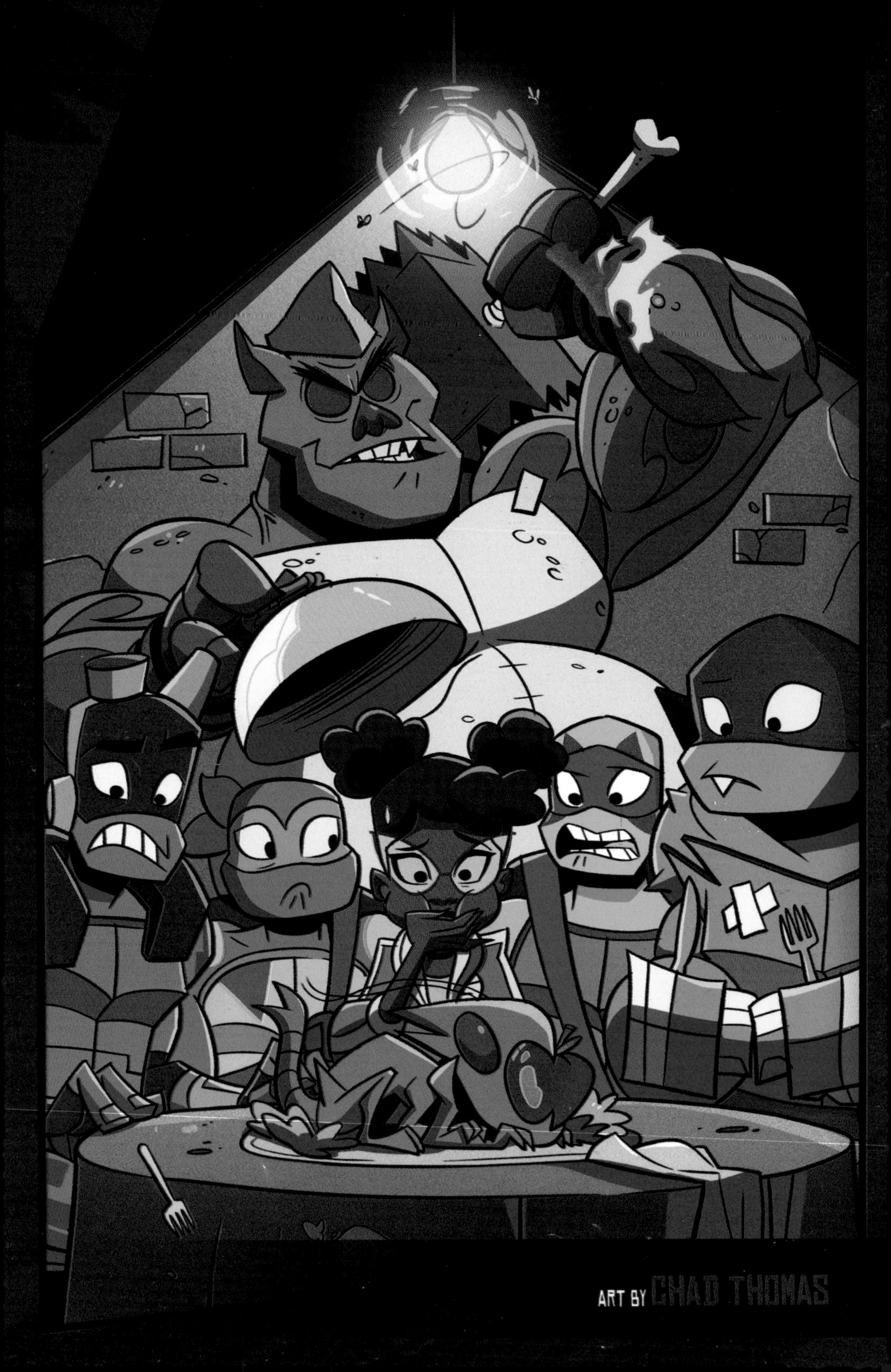

ART BY CHAD THOMAS

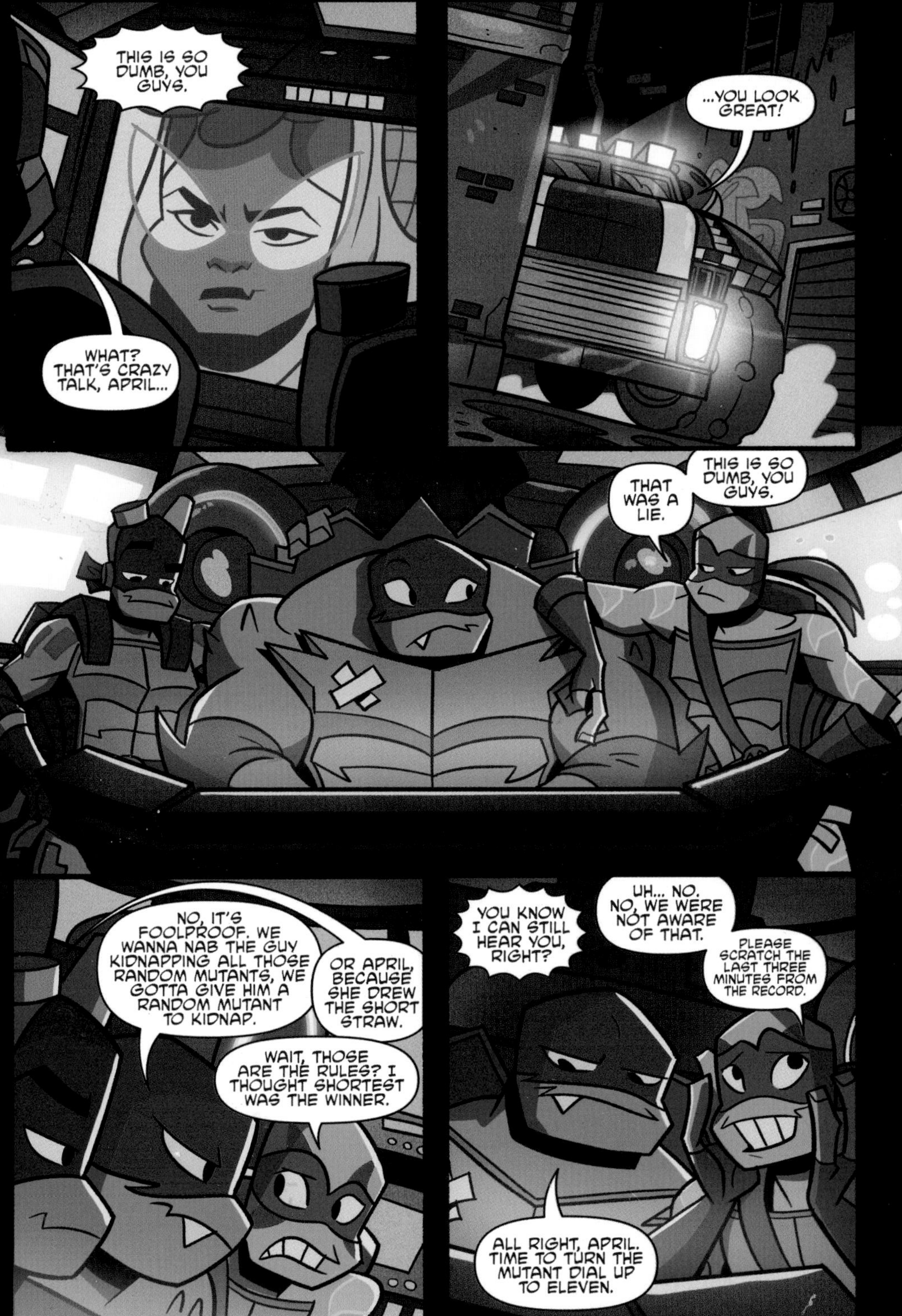
THIS IS SO DUMB, YOU GUYS.
WHAT? THAT'S CRAZY TALK, APRIL...
...YOU LOOK GREAT!
THAT WAS A LIE.
THIS IS SO DUMB, YOU GUYS.
NO, IT'S FOOLPROOF. WE WANNA NAB THE GUY KIDNAPPING ALL THOSE RANDOM MUTANTS, WE GOTTA GIVE HIM A RANDOM MUTANT TO KIDNAP.
OR APRIL, BECAUSE SHE DREW THE SHORT STRAW.
WAIT, THOSE ARE THE RULES? I THOUGHT SHORTEST WAS THE WINNER.
YOU KNOW I CAN STILL HEAR YOU, RIGHT?
UH... NO. NO, WE WERE NOT AWARE OF THAT.
PLEASE SCRATCH THE LAST THREE MINUTES FROM THE RECORD.
ALL RIGHT, APRIL. TIME TO TURN THE MUTANT DIAL UP TO ELEVEN.

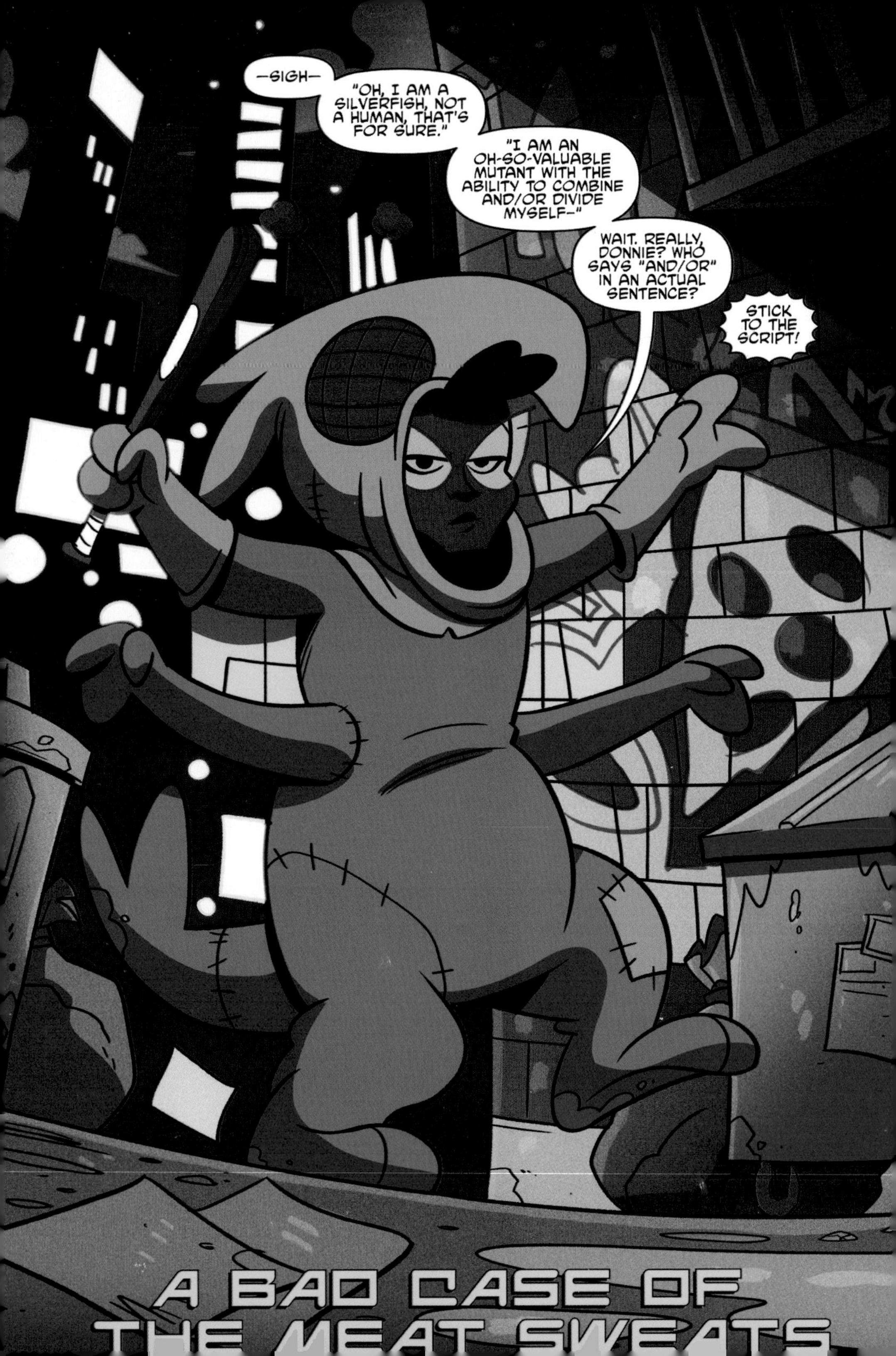
—SIGH—
"OH, I AM A SILVERFISH, NOT A HUMAN, THAT'S FOR SURE."
"I AM AN OH-SO-VALUABLE MUTANT WITH THE ABILITY TO COMBINE AND/OR DIVIDE MYSELF–"
WAIT. REALLY, DONNIE? WHO SAYS "AND/OR" IN AN ACTUAL SENTENCE?
STICK TO THE SCRIPT!
A BAD CASE OF THE MEAT SWEATS

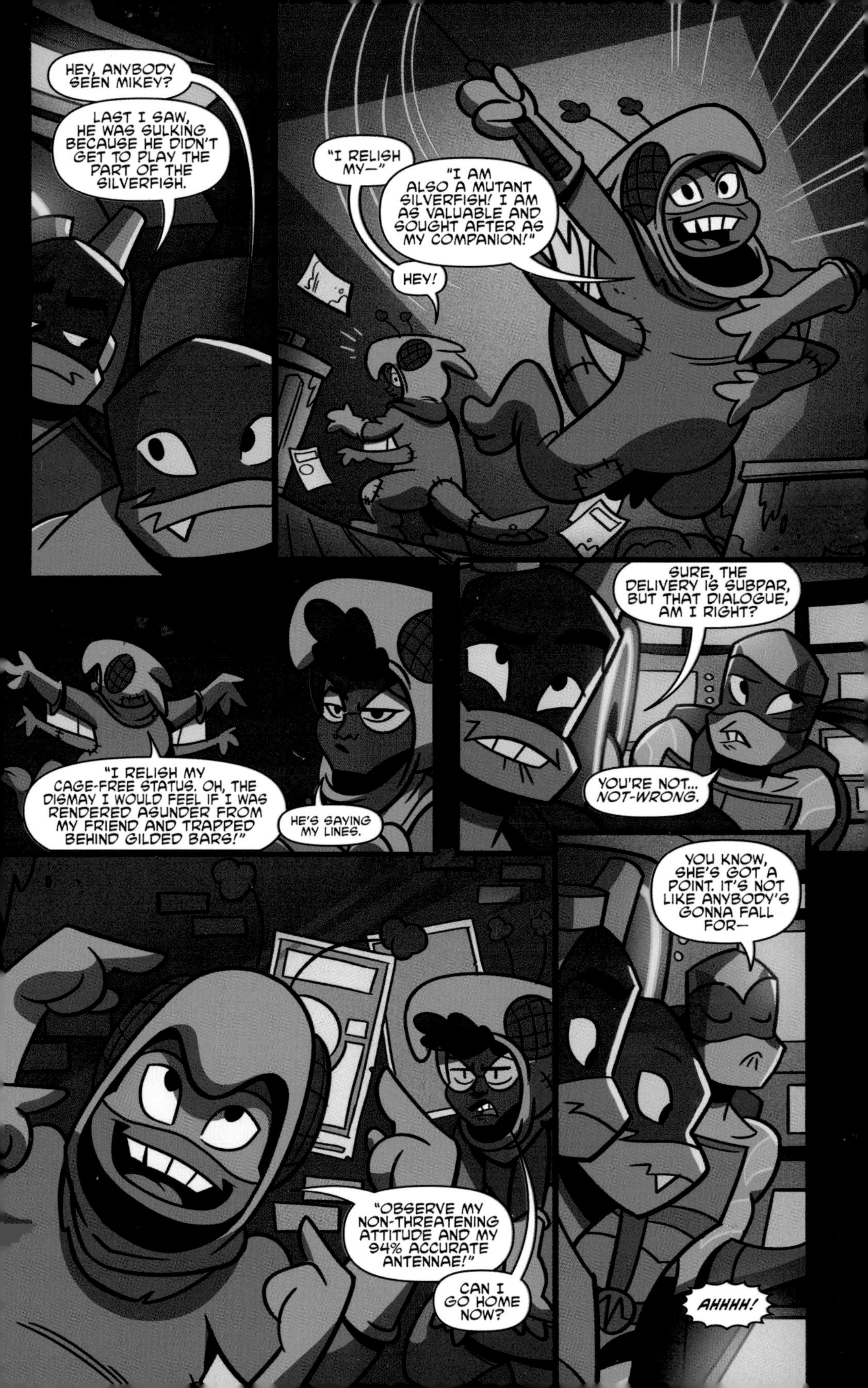
HEY, ANYBODY SEEN MIKEY?
LAST I SAW, HE WAS SULKING BECAUSE HE DIDN'T GET TO PLAY THE PART OF THE SILVERFISH.
"I RELISH MY—"
"I AM ALSO A MUTANT SILVERFISH! I AM AS VALUABLE AND SOUGHT AFTER AS MY COMPANION!"
HEY!
"I RELISH MY CAGE-FREE STATUS. OH, THE DISMAY I WOULD FEEL IF I WAS RENDERED ASUNDER FROM MY FRIEND AND TRAPPED BEHIND GILDED BARS!"
HE'S SAYING MY LINES.
SURE, THE DELIVERY IS SUBPAR, BUT THAT DIALOGUE, AM I RIGHT?
YOU'RE NOT... *NOT*-WRONG.
"OBSERVE MY NON-THREATENING ATTITUDE AND MY 94% ACCURATE ANTENNAE!"
CAN I GO HOME NOW?
YOU KNOW, SHE'S GOT A POINT. IT'S NOT LIKE ANYBODY'S GONNA FALL FOR—
AHHHH!

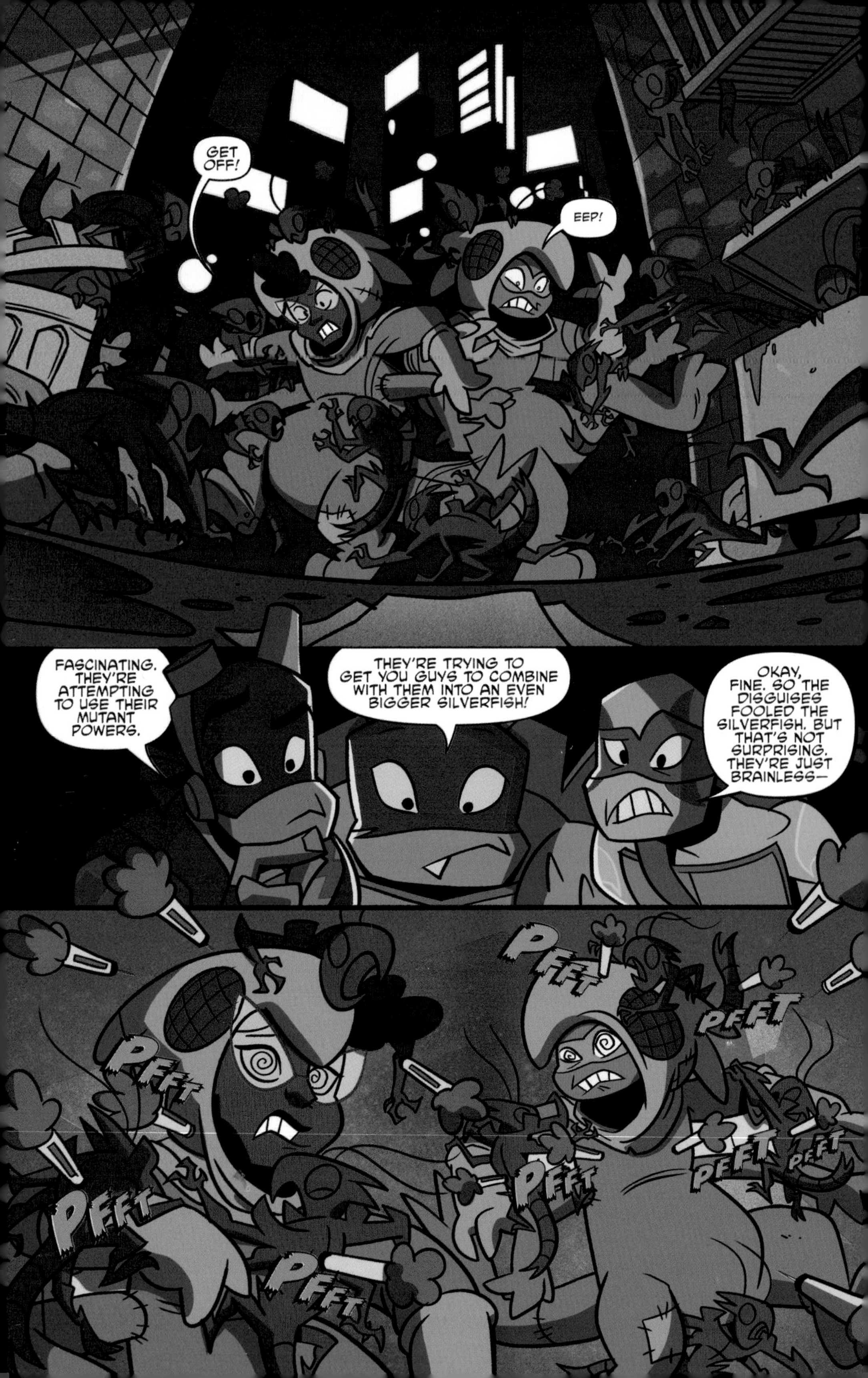
GET OFF!
EEP!
FASCINATING. THEY'RE ATTEMPTING TO USE THEIR MUTANT POWERS.
THEY'RE TRYING TO GET YOU GUYS TO COMBINE WITH THEM INTO AN EVEN BIGGER SILVERFISH!
OKAY, FINE. SO THE DISGUISES FOOLED THE SILVERFISH. BUT THAT'S NOT SURPRISING. THEY'RE JUST BRAINLESS—
PFFT
PFFT
PFFT
PFFT
PFFT
PFFT
PFFT
PFFT

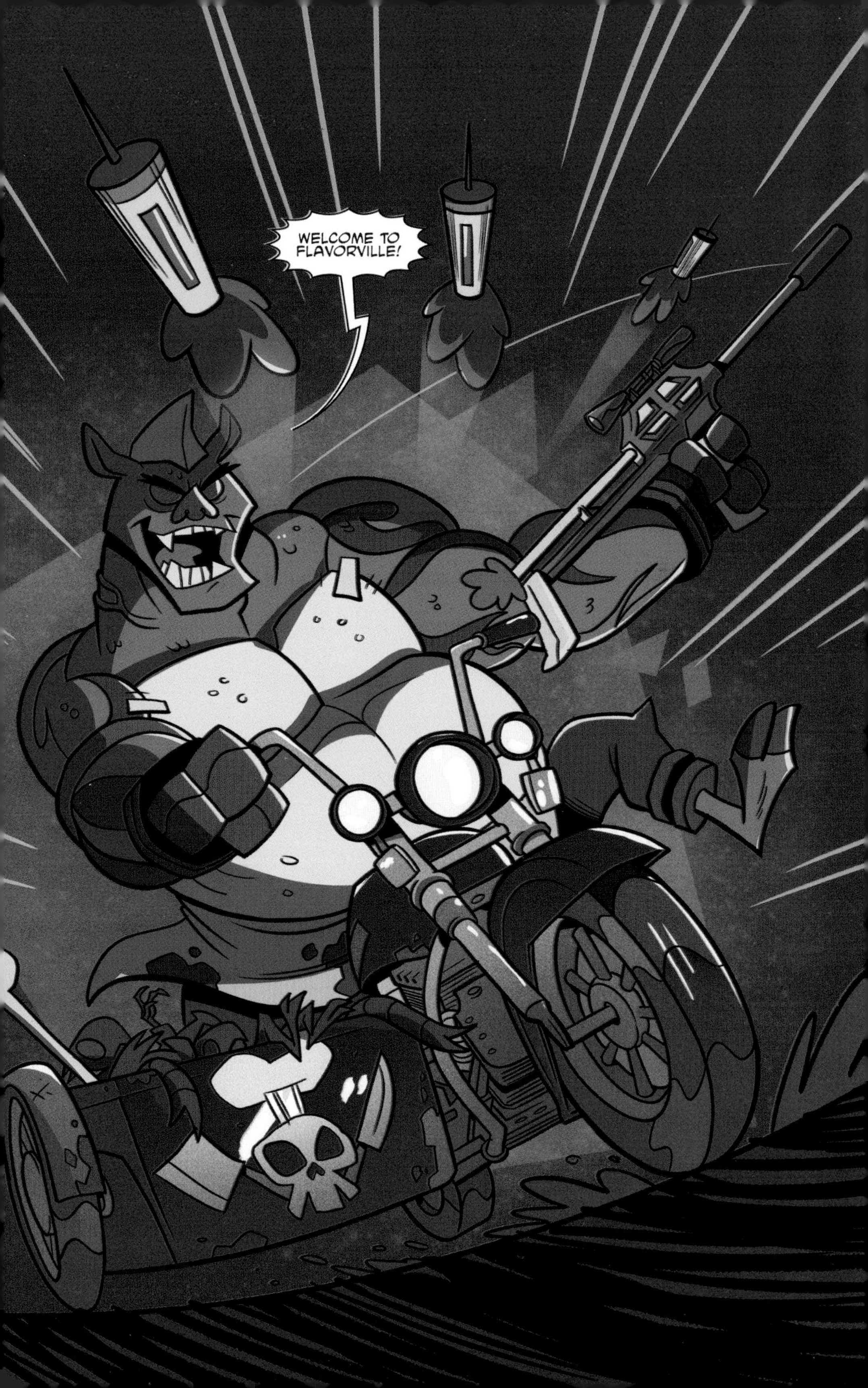
WELCOME TO FLAVORVILLE!

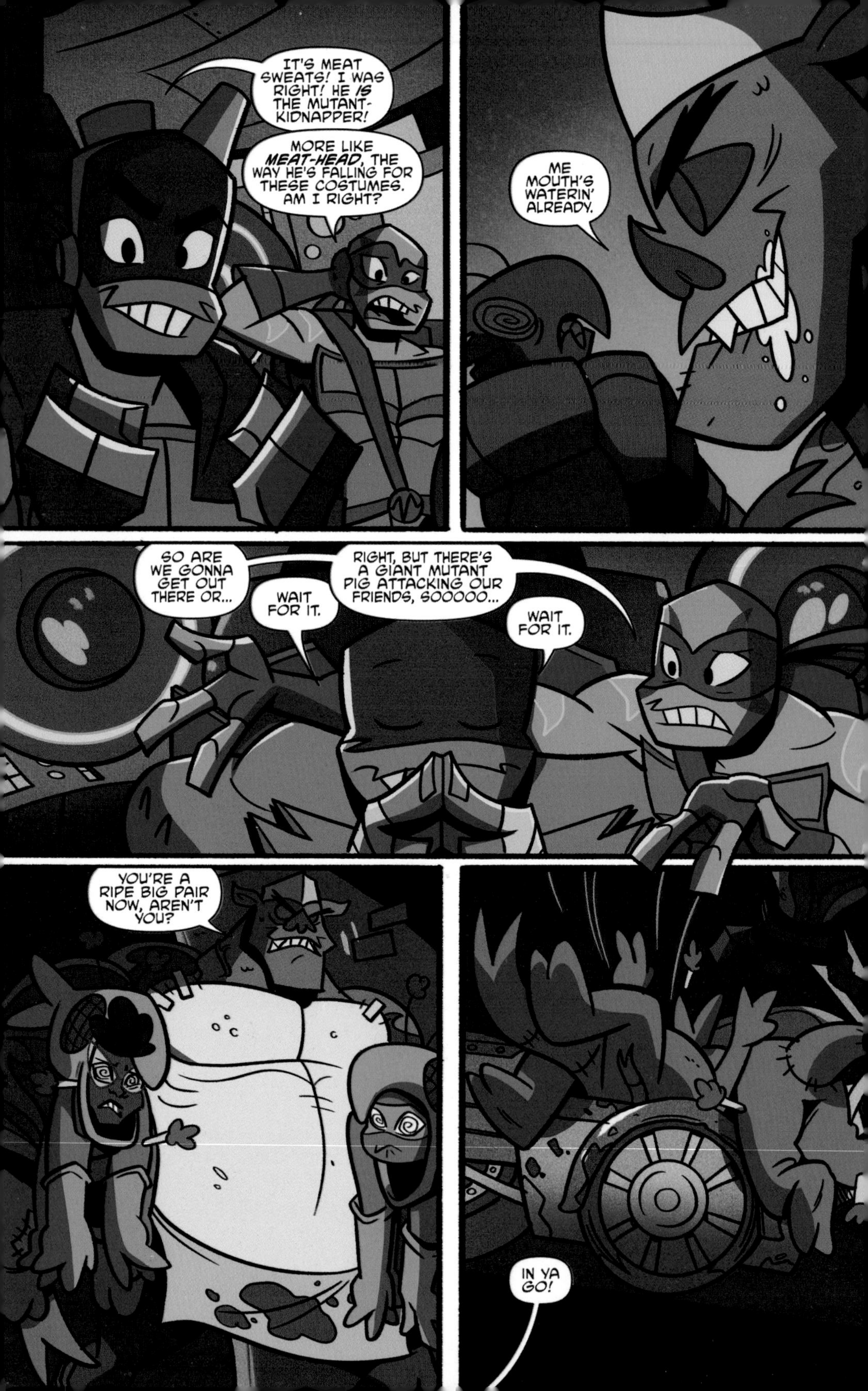
IT'S MEAT SWEATS! I WAS RIGHT! HE IS THE MUTANT-KIDNAPPER!
MORE LIKE MEAT-HEAD, THE WAY HE'S FALLING FOR THESE COSTUMES. AM I RIGHT?
ME MOUTH'S WATERIN' ALREADY.
SO ARE WE GONNA GET OUT THERE OR...
WAIT FOR IT.
RIGHT, BUT THERE'S A GIANT MUTANT PIG ATTACKING OUR FRIENDS, SOOOOO...
WAIT FOR IT.
YOU'RE A RIPE BIG PAIR NOW, AREN'T YOU?
IN YA GO!

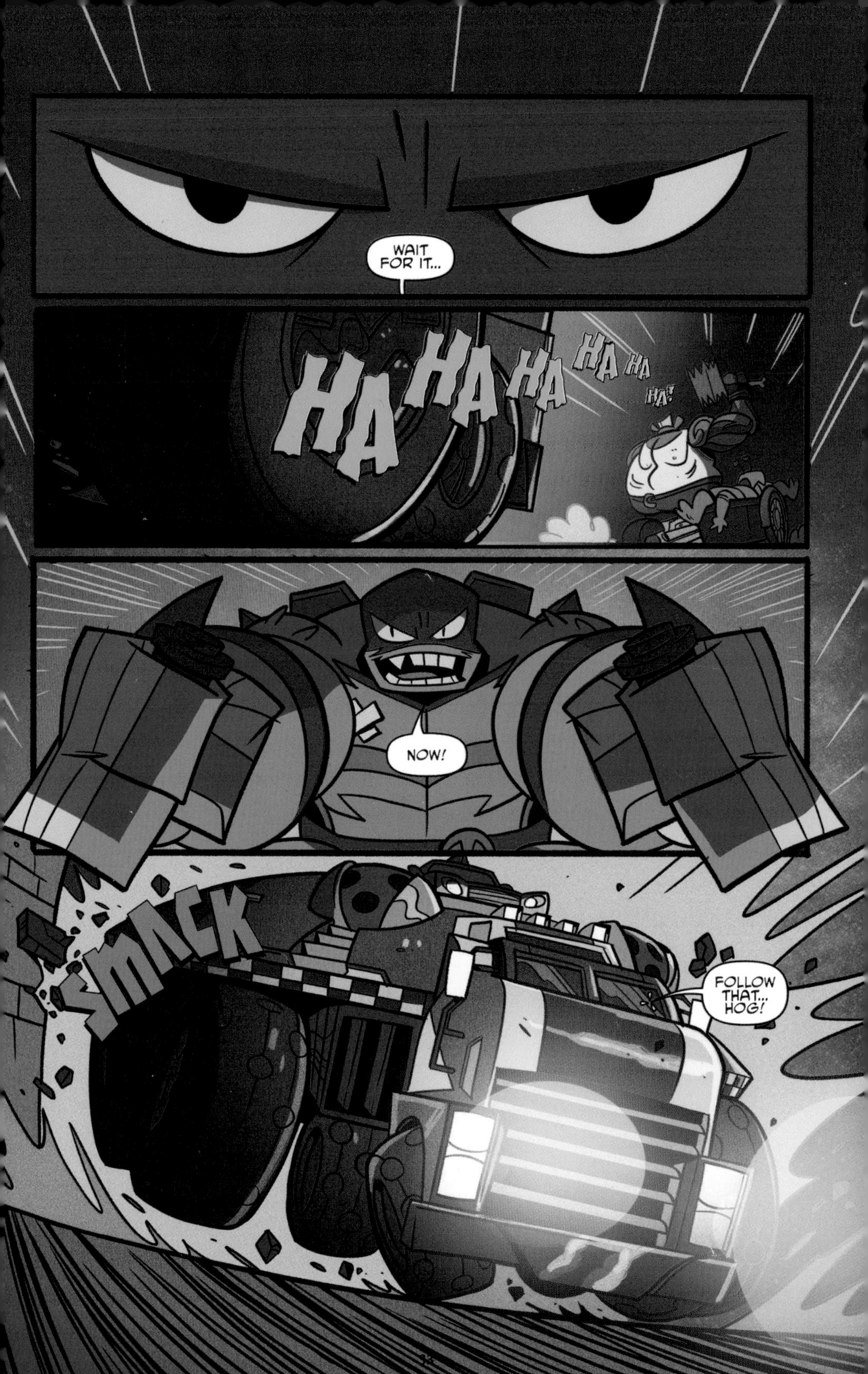
WAIT FOR IT...
HA HA HA HA HA HA HA!
NOW!
SMACK
FOLLOW THAT... HOG!

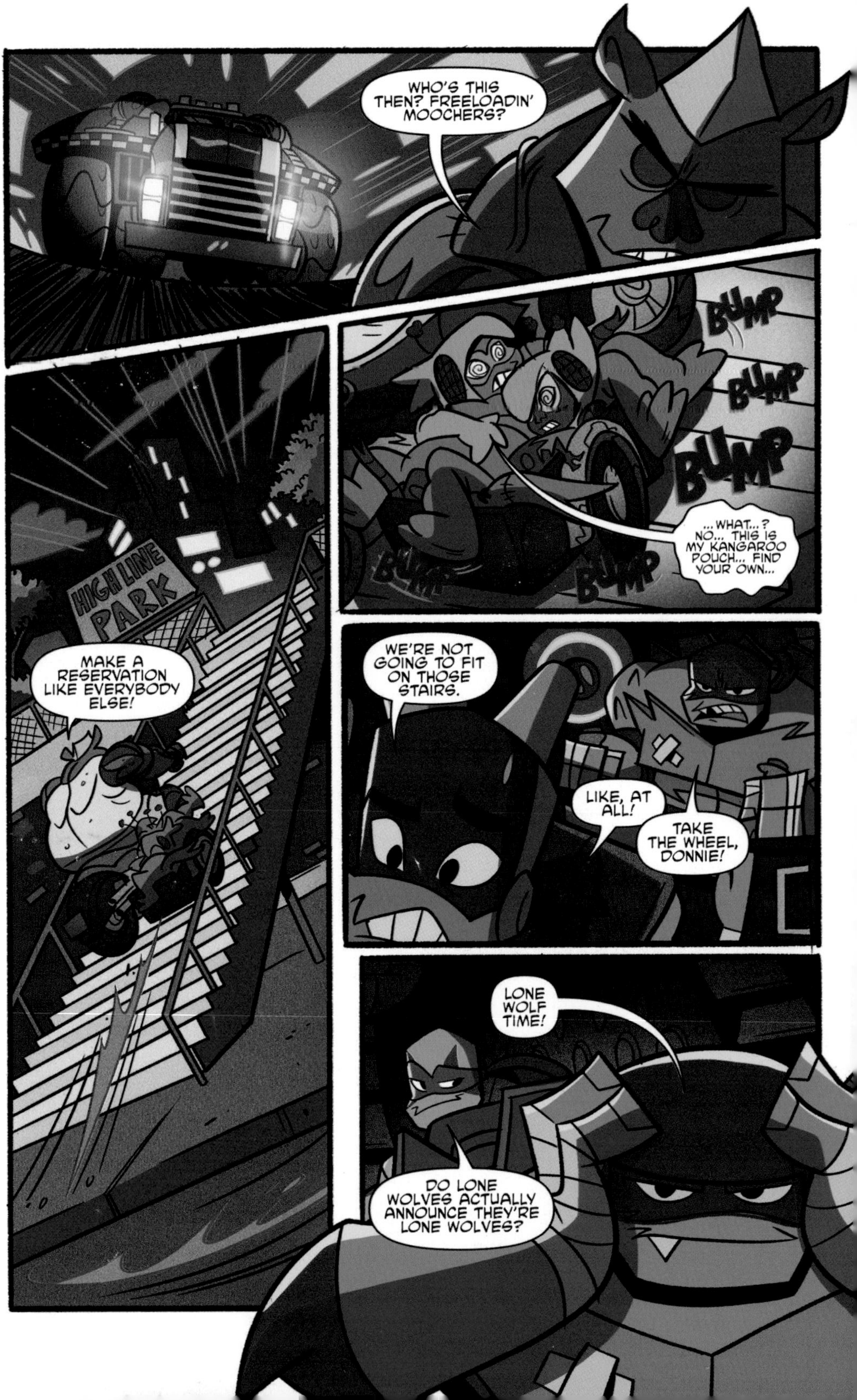
WHO'S THIS THEN? FREELOADIN' MOOCHERS?
BUMP
BUMP
BUMP
...WHAT...? NO... THIS IS MY KANGAROO POUCH... FIND YOUR OWN...
HIGH LINE PARK
MAKE A RESERVATION LIKE EVERYBODY ELSE!
WE'RE NOT GOING TO FIT ON THOSE STAIRS.
LIKE, AT ALL!
TAKE THE WHEEL, DONNIE!
LONE WOLF TIME!
DO LONE WOLVES ACTUALLY ANNOUNCE THEY'RE LONE WOLVES?

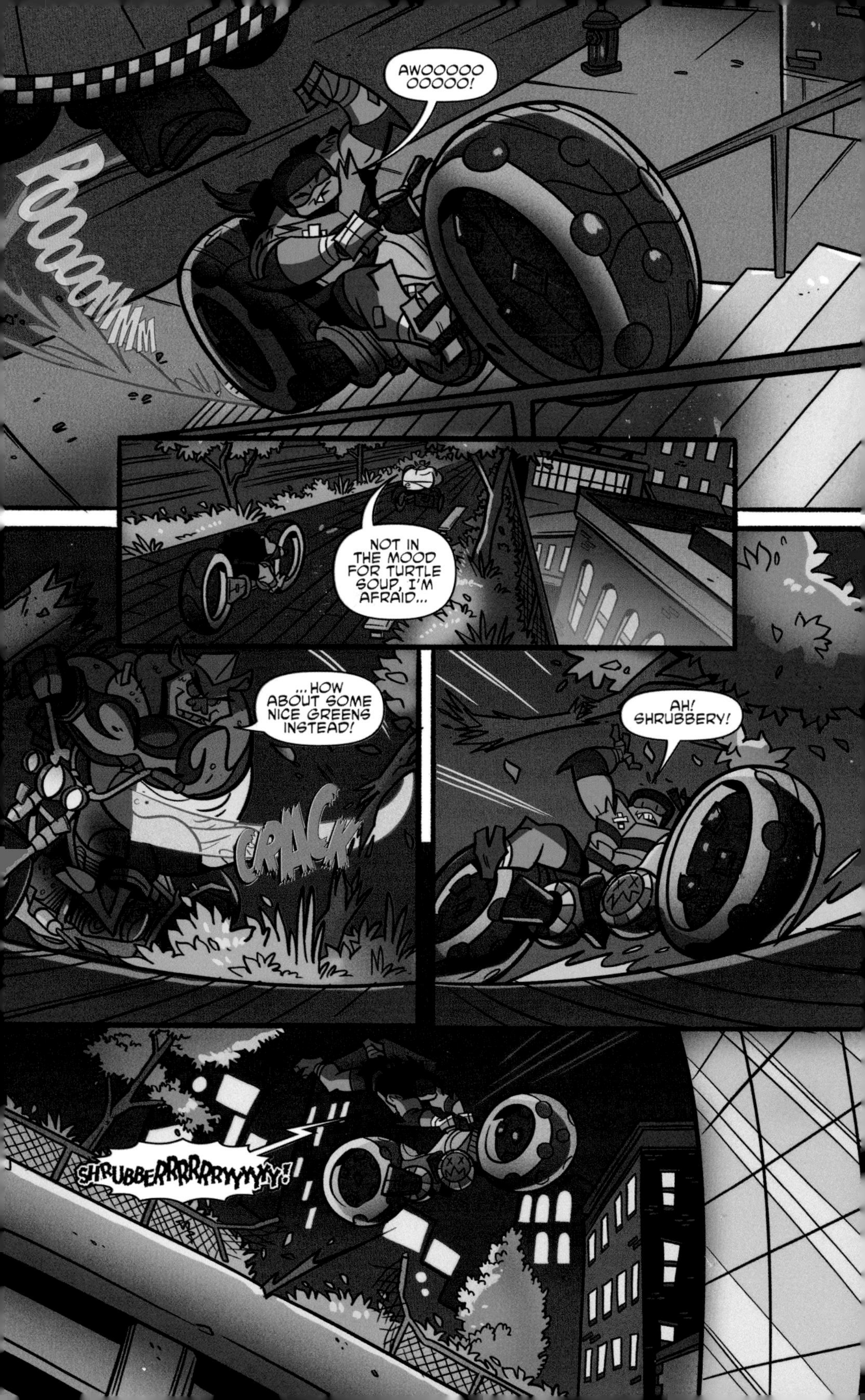
AWOOOOO OOOOO!
BOOOOOMMM
NOT IN THE MOOD FOR TURTLE SOUP, I'M AFRAID...
...HOW ABOUT SOME NICE GREENS INSTEAD!
CRACK
AH! SHRUBBERY!
SHRUBBERRRRRRYYYYY!

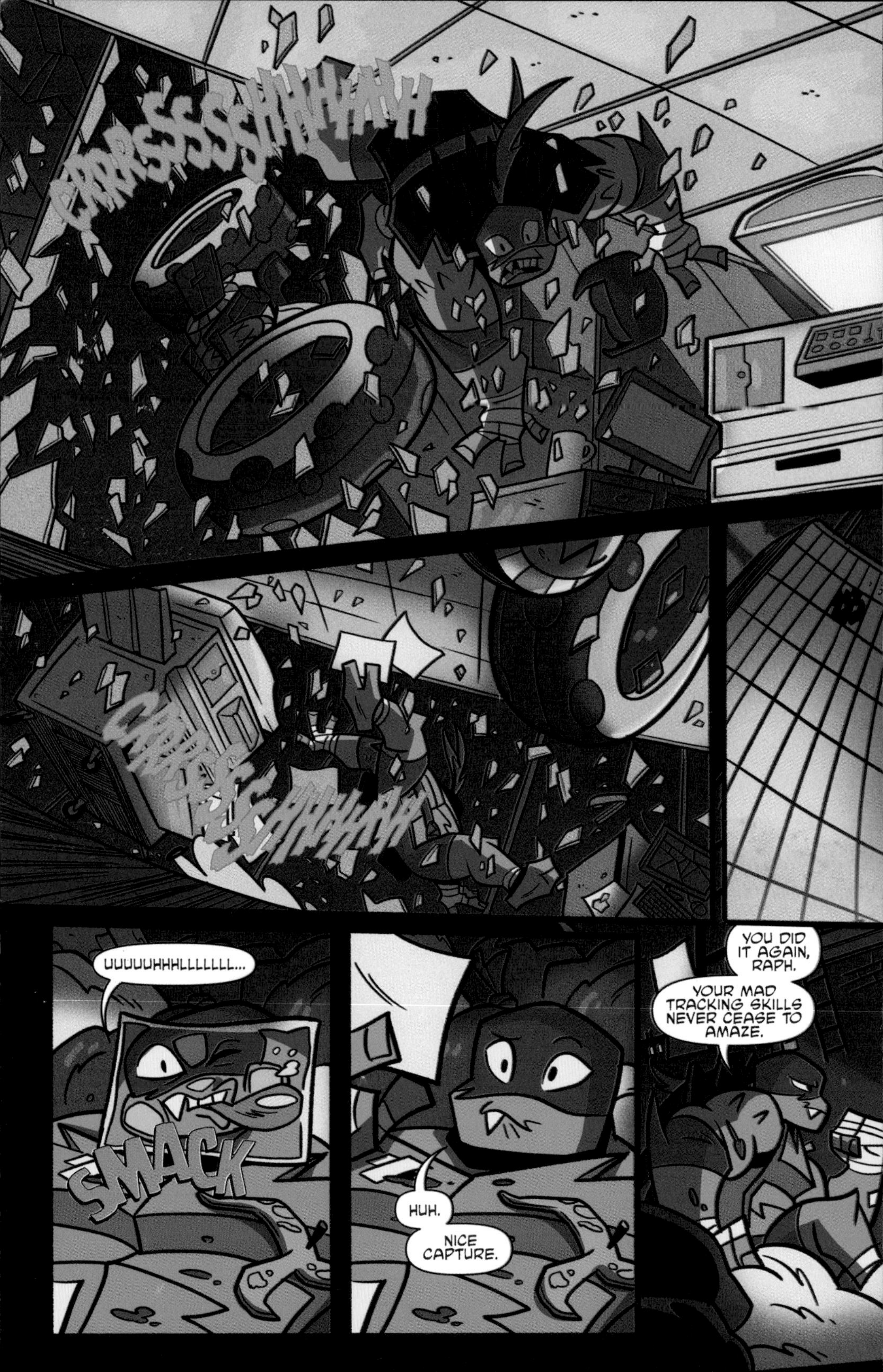
CRRRSSSSHHHHHH
CRRSSSSHHHHHH
UUUUUHHHLLLLLLL...
SMACK
HUH.
NICE CAPTURE.
YOU DID IT AGAIN, RAPH.
YOUR MAD TRACKING SKILLS NEVER CEASE TO AMAZE.

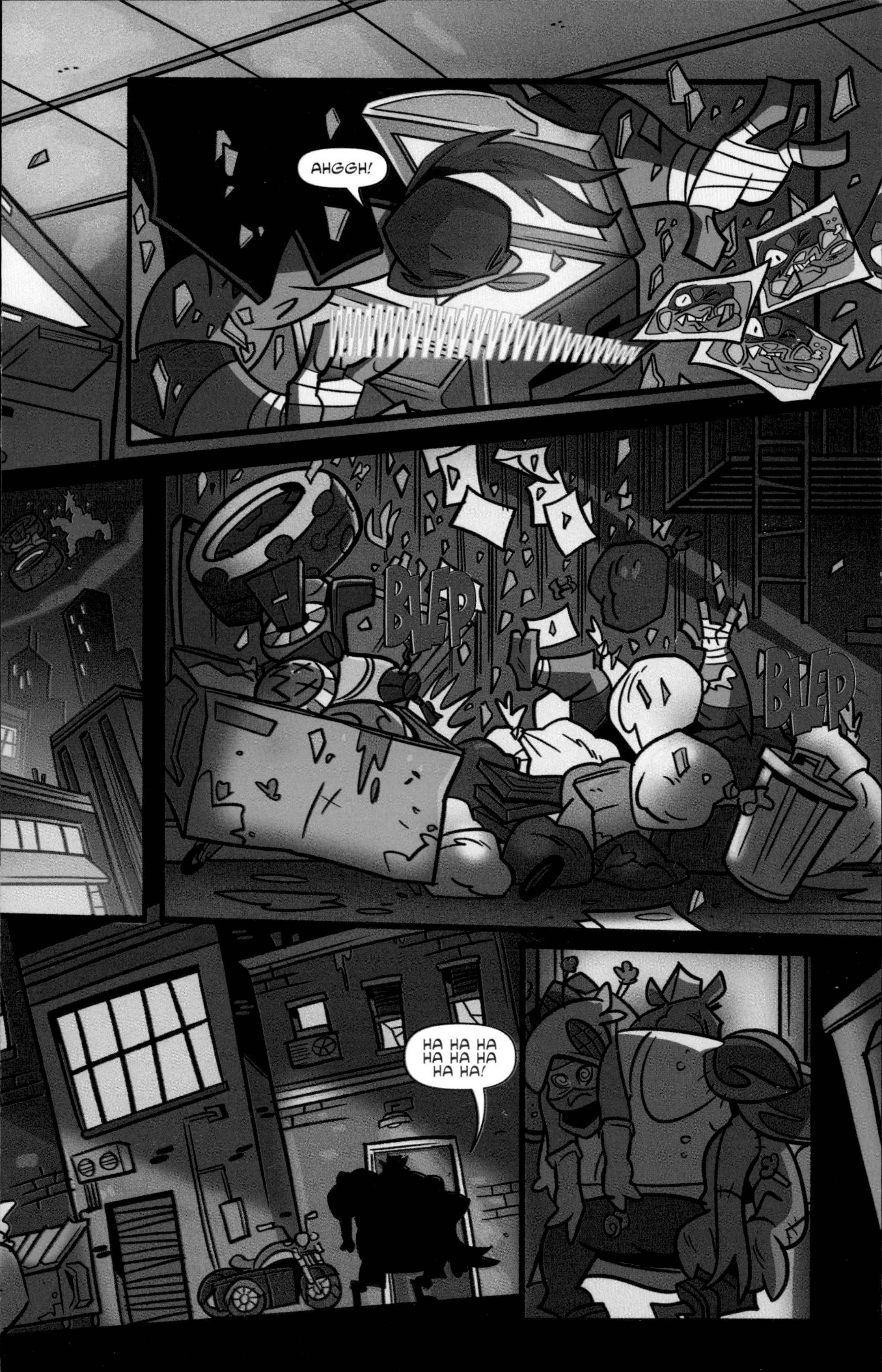
AHGGH!
BLLEP
BLLEP
HA HA HA
HA HA HA
HA HA!

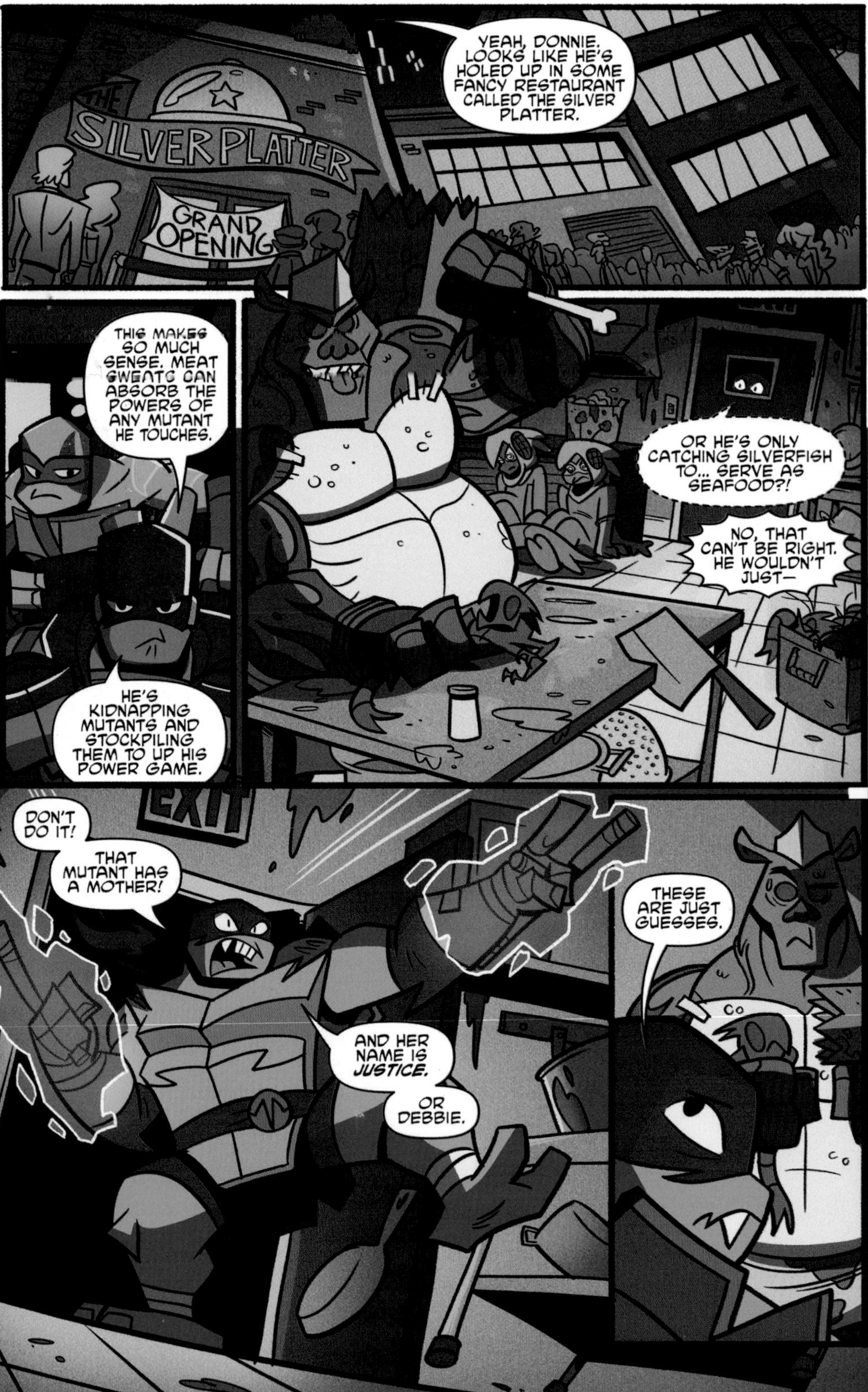
THE SILVER PLATTER
GRAND OPENING
YEAH, DONNIE. LOOKS LIKE HE'S HOLED UP IN SOME FANCY RESTAURANT CALLED THE SILVER PLATTER.
THIS MAKES SO MUCH SENSE. MEAT SWEATS CAN ABSORB THE POWERS OF ANY MUTANT HE TOUCHES.
HE'S KIDNAPPING MUTANTS AND STOCKPILING THEM TO UP HIS POWER GAME.
OR HE'S ONLY CATCHING SILVERFISH TO... SERVE AS SEAFOOD?!
NO, THAT CAN'T BE RIGHT. HE WOULDN'T JUST—
EXIT
DON'T DO IT!
THAT MUTANT HAS A MOTHER!
AND HER NAME IS *JUSTICE.*
OR DEBBIE.
THESE ARE JUST GUESSES.

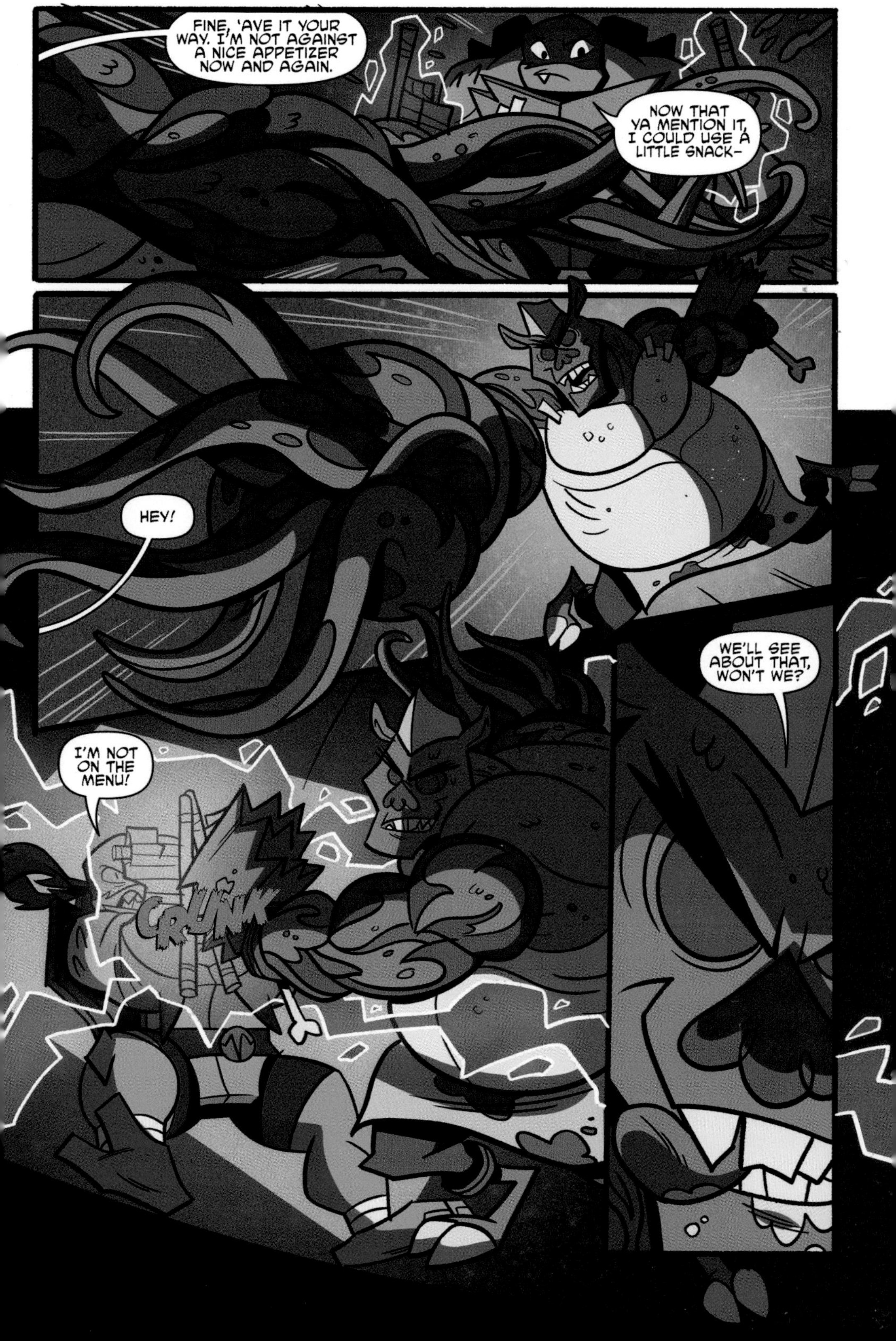
FINE, 'AVE IT YOUR WAY. I'M NOT AGAINST A NICE APPETIZER NOW AND AGAIN.
NOW THAT YA MENTION IT, I COULD USE A LITTLE SNACK-
HEY!
WE'LL SEE ABOUT THAT, WON'T WE?
I'M NOT ON THE MENU!
CRUNK

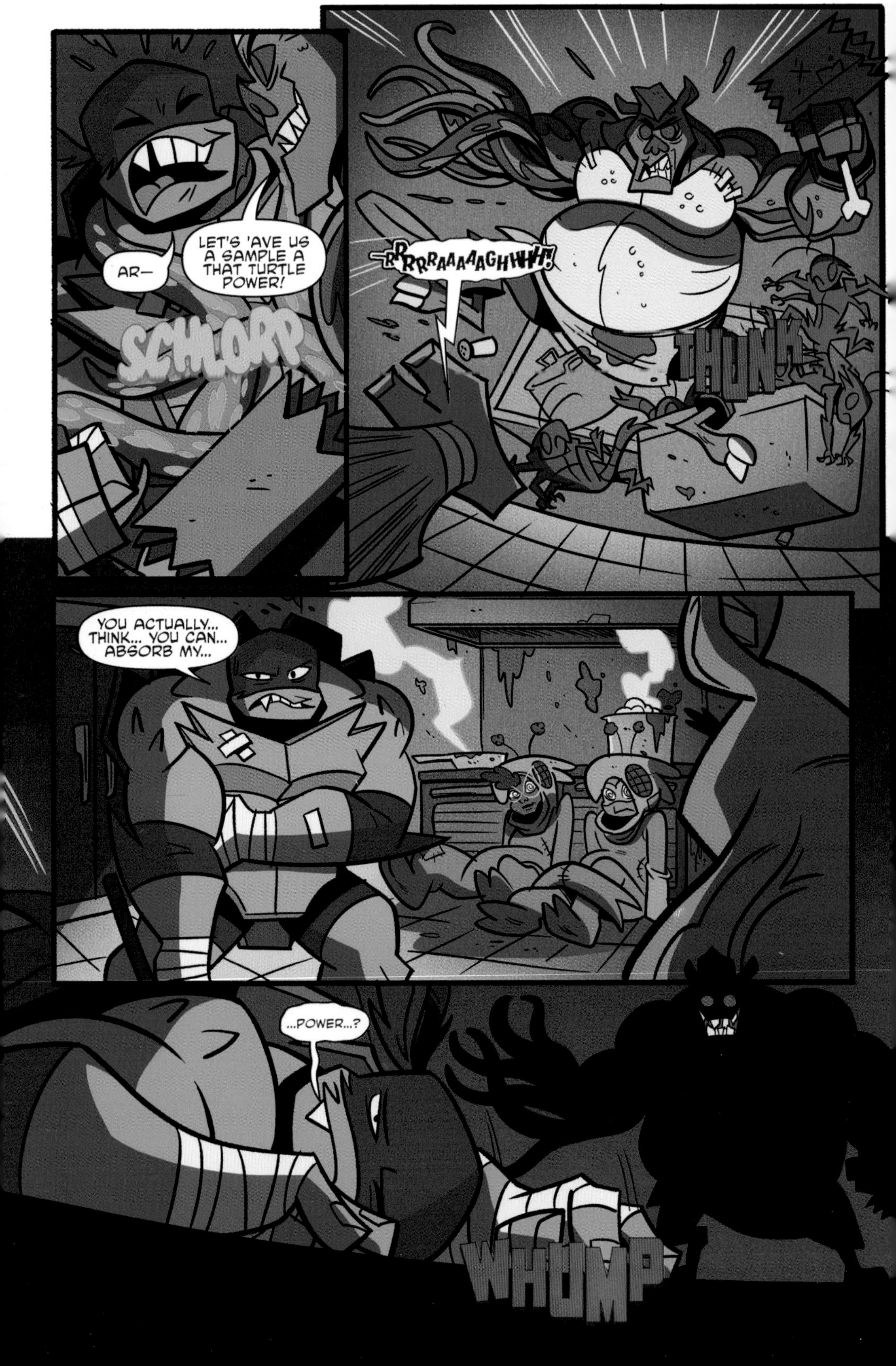
AR—
LET'S 'AVE US A SAMPLE A THAT TURTLE POWER!
SCHLORP
RRRRAAAAAGHHH!
THUNK
YOU ACTUALLY... THINK... YOU CAN... ABSORB MY...
...POWER...?
WHUMP

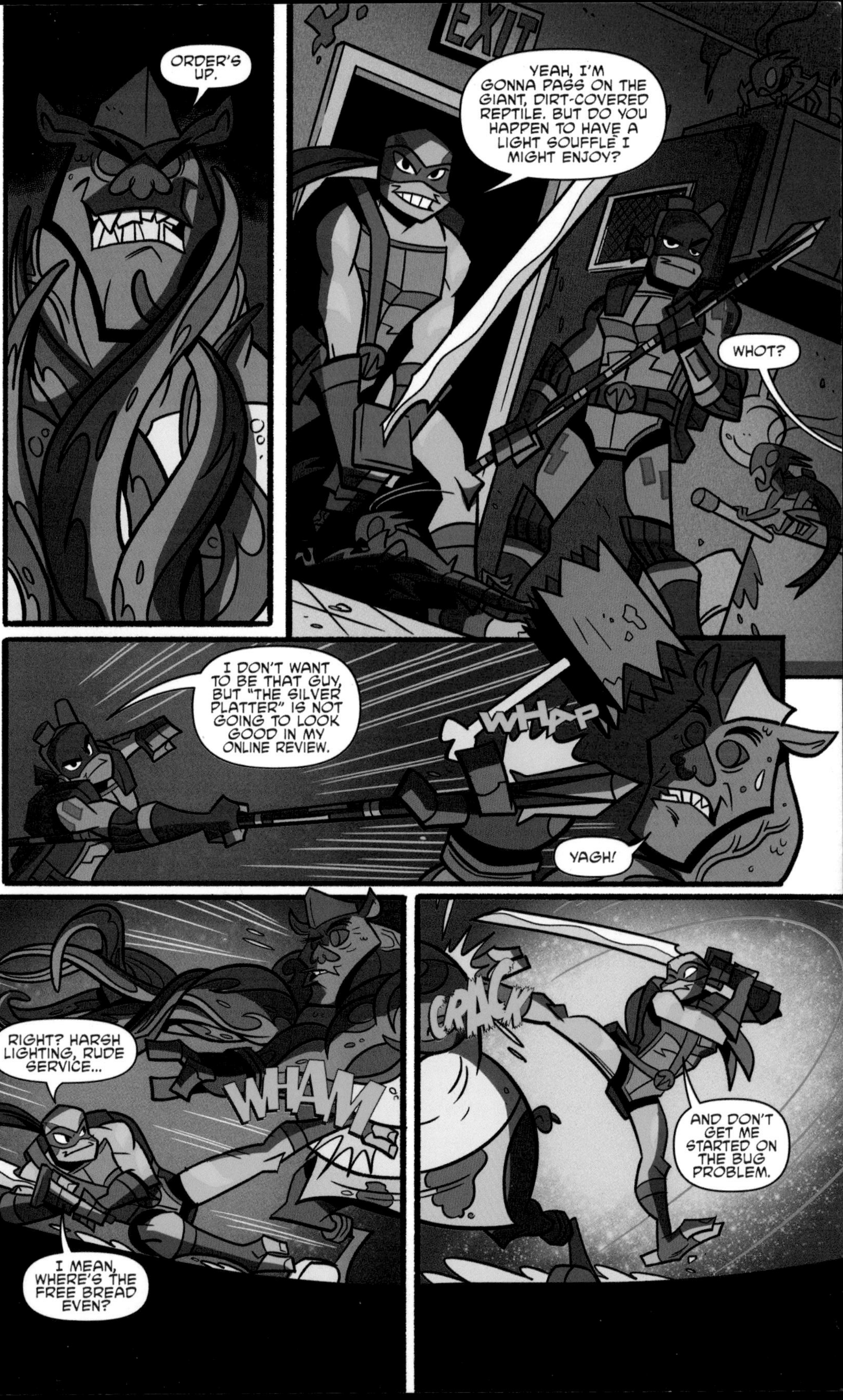
ORDER'S UP.
YEAH, I'M GONNA PASS ON THE GIANT, DIRT-COVERED REPTILE. BUT DO YOU HAPPEN TO HAVE A LIGHT SOUFFLÉ I MIGHT ENJOY?
WHOT?
I DON'T WANT TO BE THAT GUY, BUT "THE SILVER PLATTER" IS NOT GOING TO LOOK GOOD IN MY ONLINE REVIEW.
WHAP
YAGH!
RIGHT? HARSH LIGHTING, RUDE SERVICE...
WHAM
I MEAN, WHERE'S THE FREE BREAD EVEN?
CRACK
AND DON'T GET ME STARTED ON THE BUG PROBLEM.

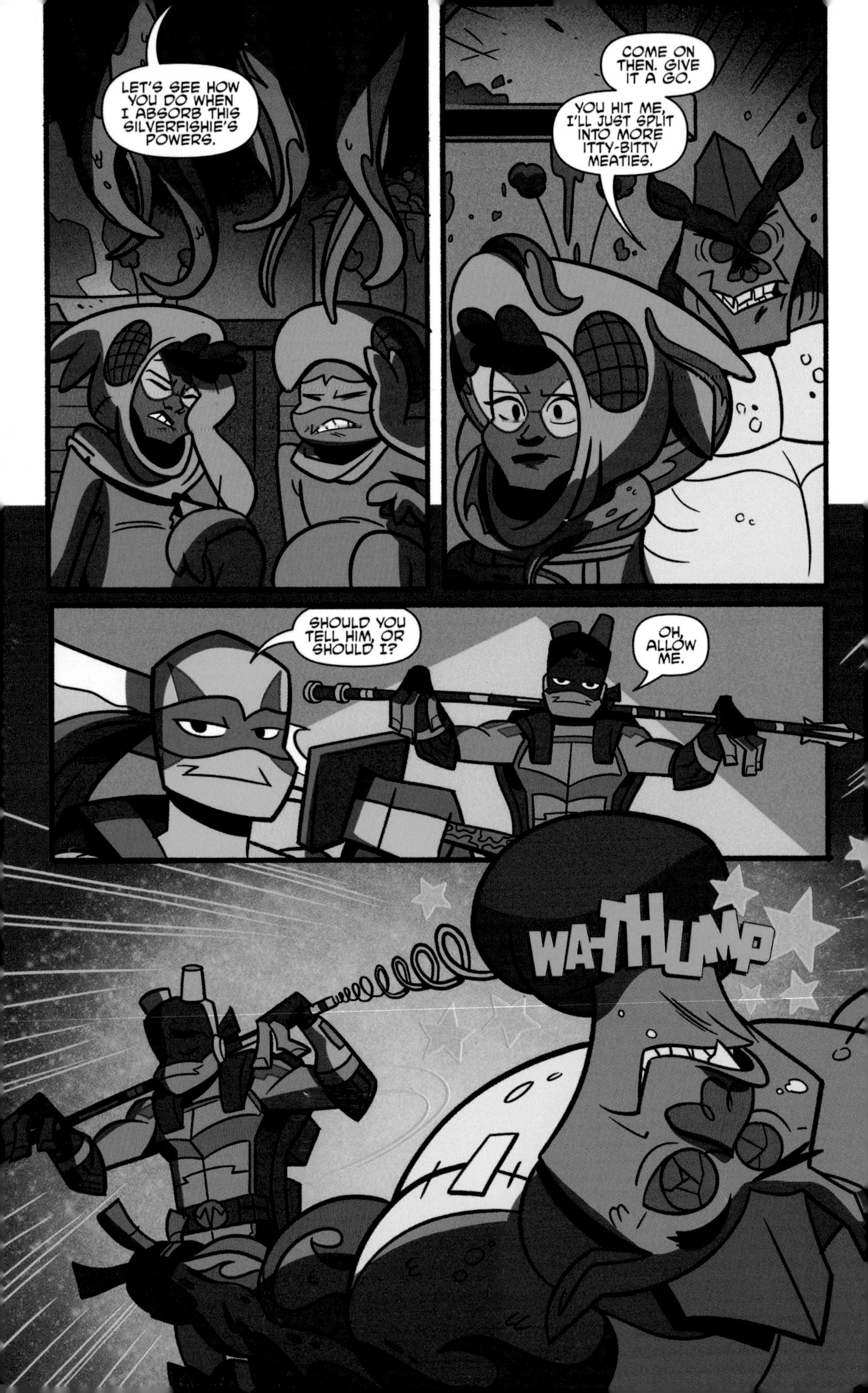
LET'S SEE HOW YOU DO WHEN I ABSORB THIS SILVERFISHIE'S POWERS.
COME ON THEN. GIVE IT A GO.
YOU HIT ME, I'LL JUST SPLIT INTO MORE ITTY-BITTY MEATIES.
SHOULD YOU TELL HIM, OR SHOULD I?
OH, ALLOW ME.
WA-THUMP

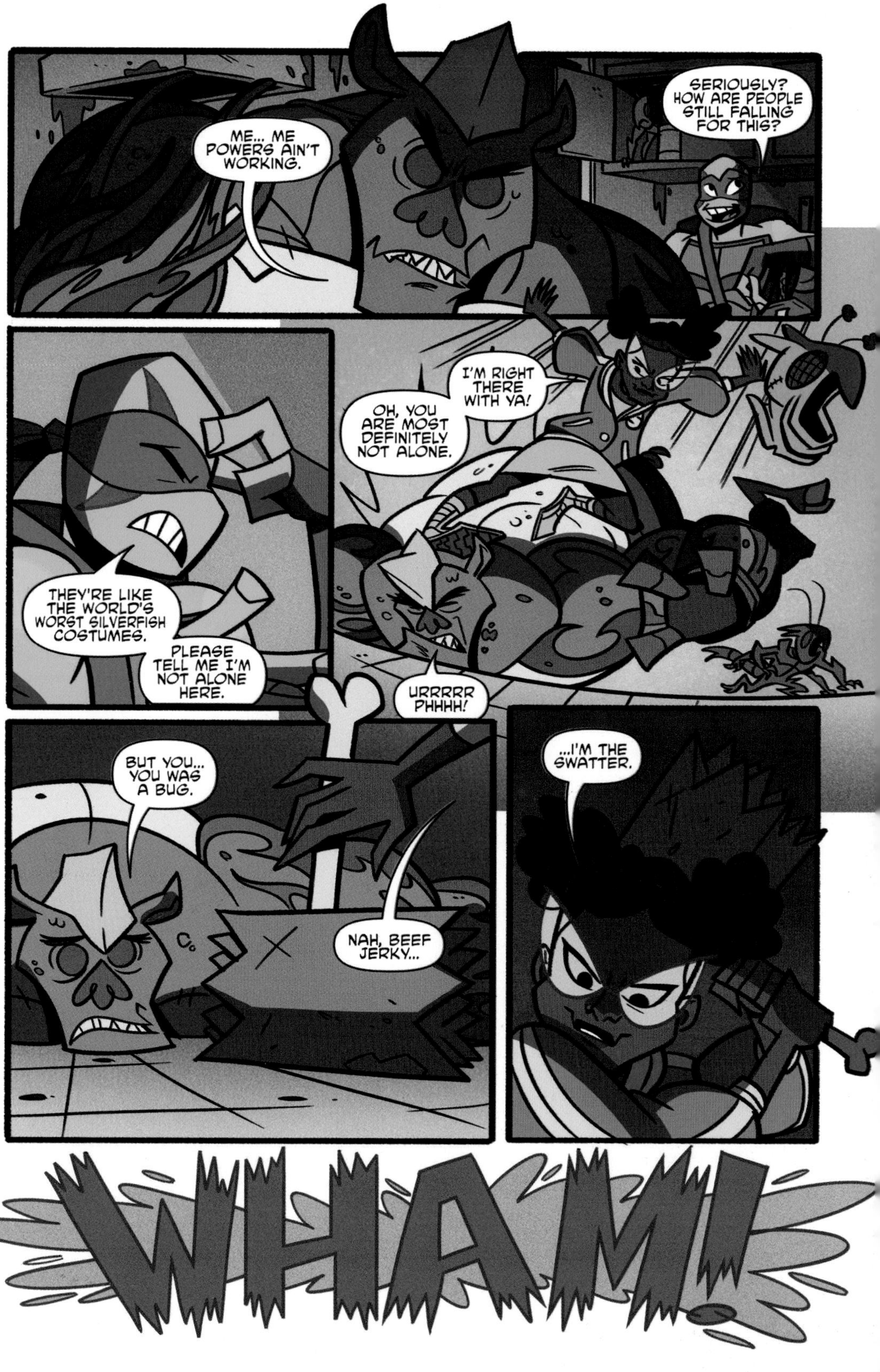
ME... ME POWERS AIN'T WORKING.
SERIOUSLY? HOW ARE PEOPLE STILL FALLING FOR THIS?
THEY'RE LIKE THE WORLD'S WORST SILVERFISH COSTUMES.
PLEASE TELL ME I'M NOT ALONE HERE.
I'M RIGHT THERE WITH YA!
OH, YOU ARE MOST DEFINITELY NOT ALONE.
URRRRR PHHHH!
BUT YOU... YOU WAS A BUG.
NAH, BEEF JERKY...
...I'M THE SWATTER.
WHAM!

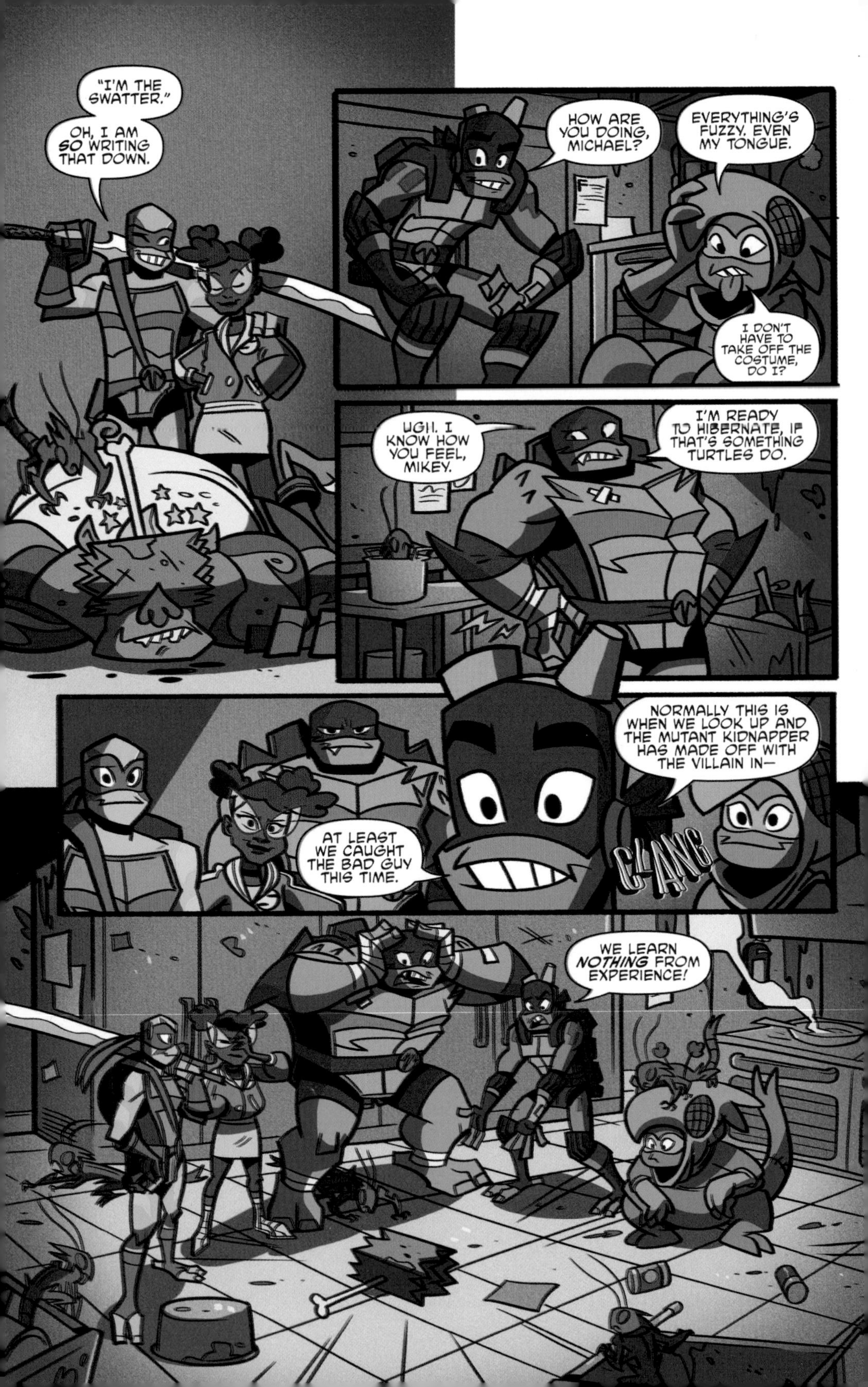
"I'M THE SWATTER."
OH, I AM *SO* WRITING THAT DOWN.
HOW ARE YOU DOING, MICHAEL?
EVERYTHING'S FUZZY. EVEN MY TONGUE.
I DON'T HAVE TO TAKE OFF THE COSTUME, DO I?
I'M READY TO HIBERNATE, IF THAT'S SOMETHING TURTLES DO.
UGH. I KNOW HOW YOU FEEL, MIKEY.
AT LEAST WE CAUGHT THE BAD GUY THIS TIME.
NORMALLY THIS IS WHEN WE LOOK UP AND THE MUTANT KIDNAPPER HAS MADE OFF WITH THE VILLAIN IN—
CLANG
WE LEARN *NOTHING* FROM EXPERIENCE!

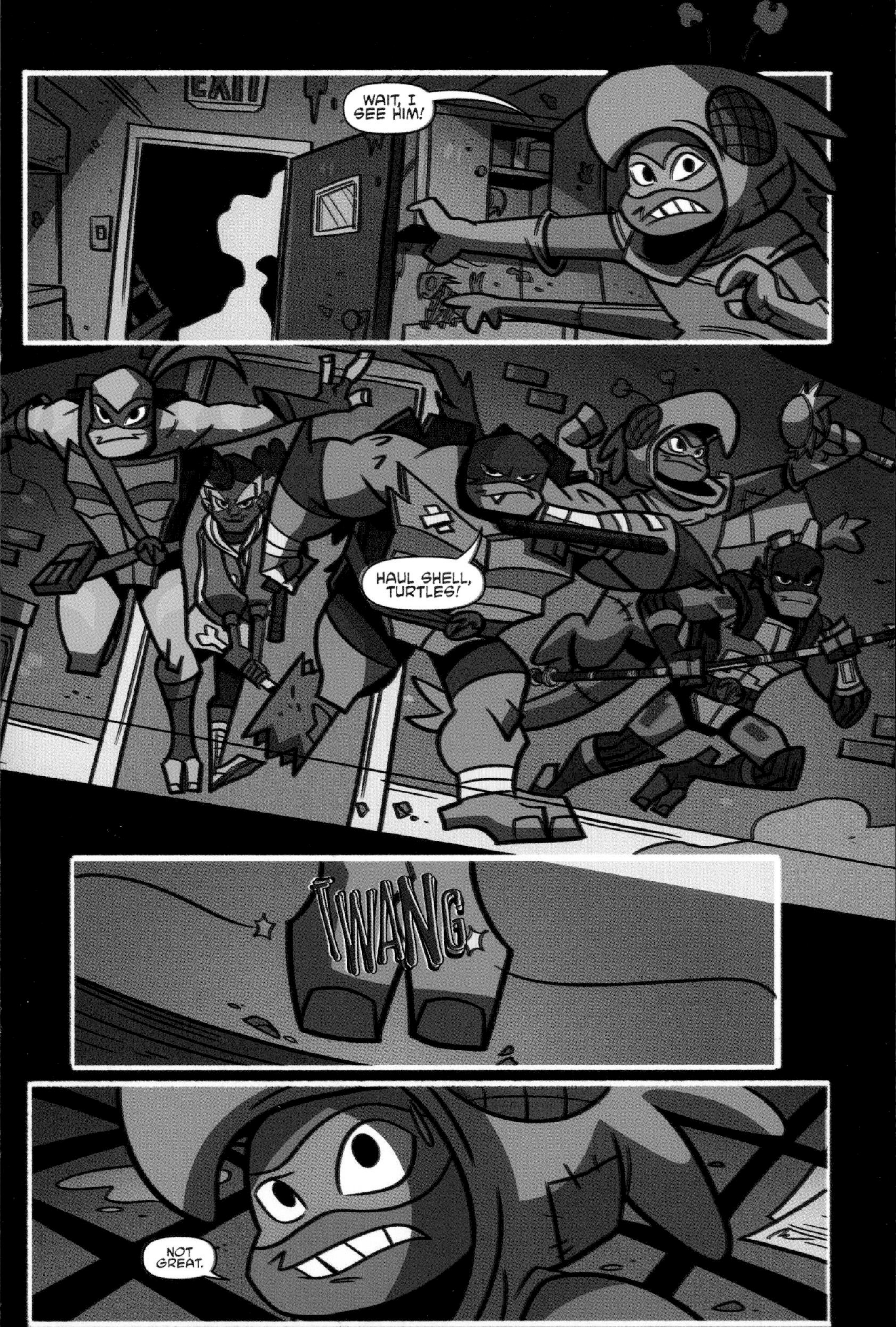

EXIT
WAIT, I SEE HIM!
HAUL SHELL, TURTLES!
TWANG
NOT GREAT.

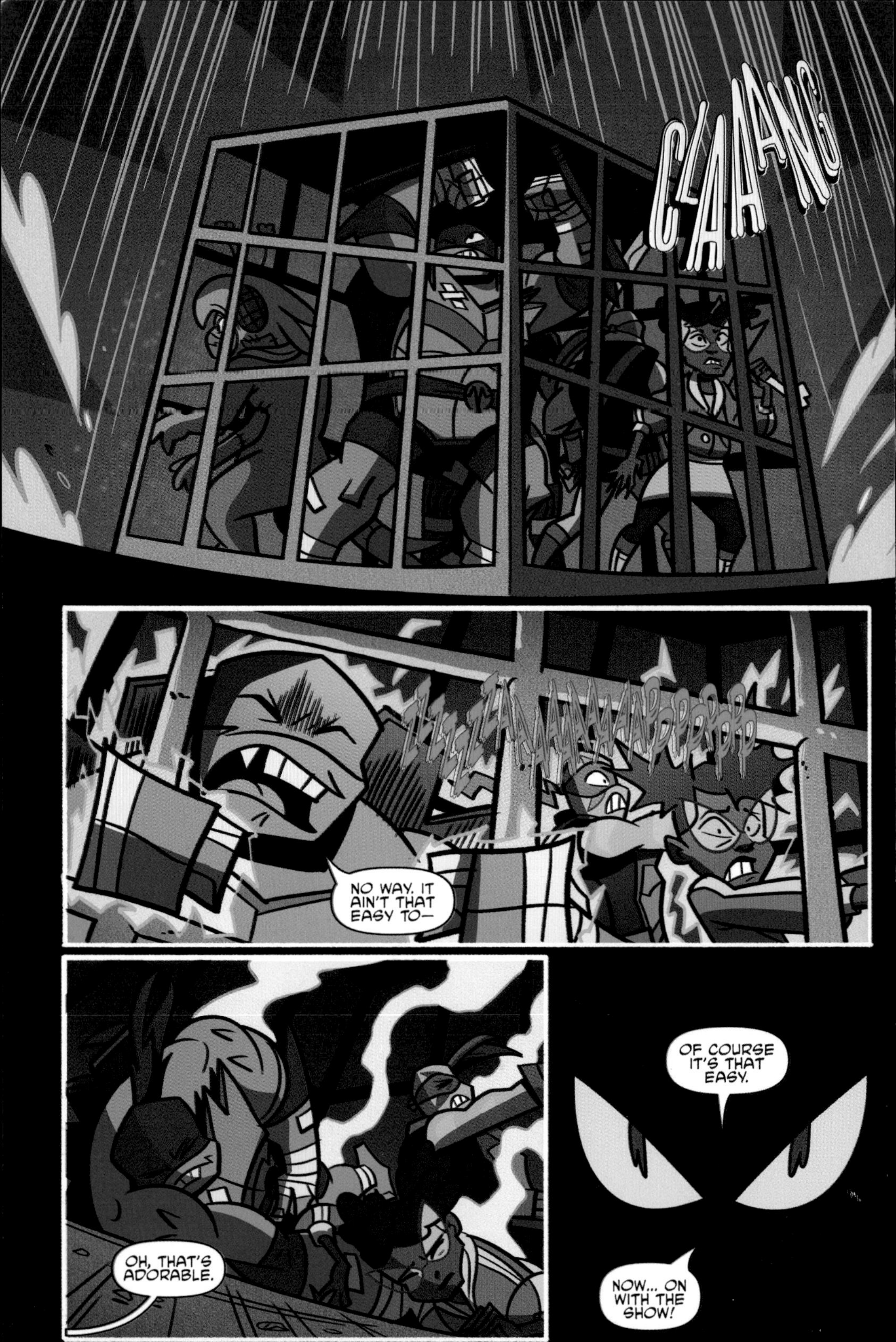
CLAAANG
ZZZZZZAAAAAAAAAAPPPPPPP
NO WAY. IT AIN'T THAT EASY TO—
OH, THAT'S ADORABLE.
OF COURSE IT'S THAT EASY.
NOW... ON WITH THE SHOW!

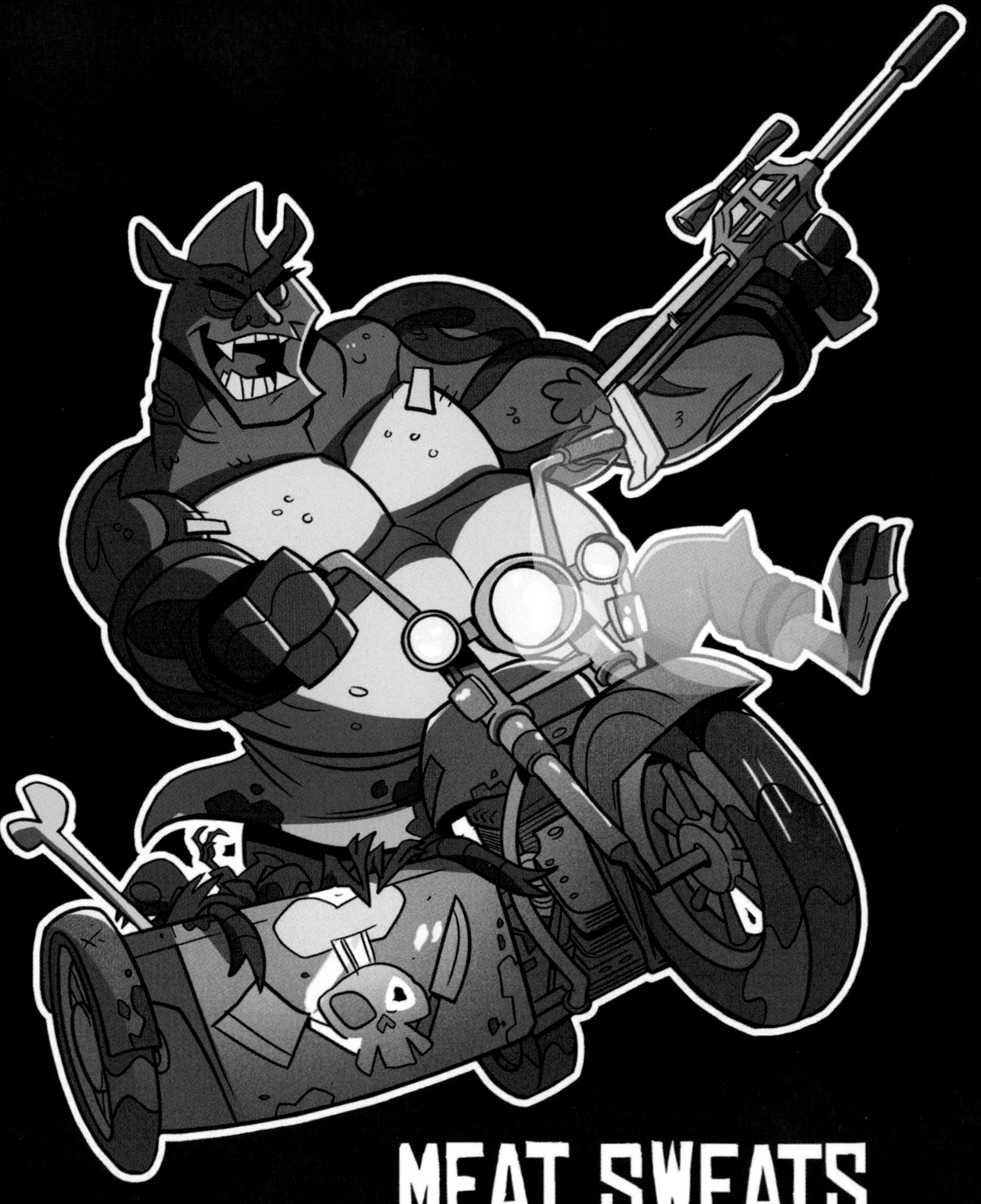

MEAT SWEATS

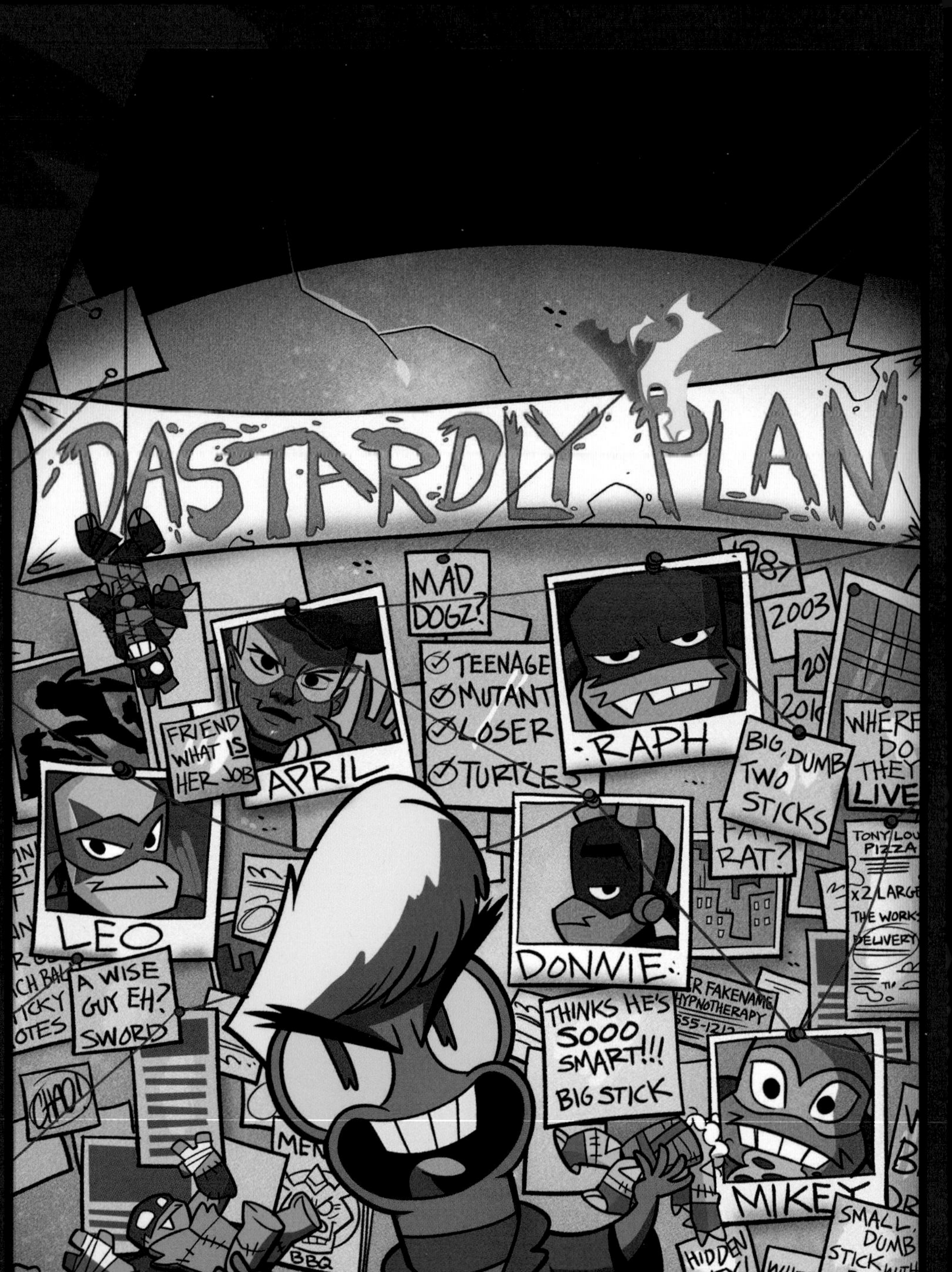
DASTARDLY PLAN
MAD DOGZ?
TEENAGE
MUTANT
LOSER
TURTLES
1987
2003
APRIL
FRIEND WHAT IS HER JOB
RAPH
BIG, DUMB TWO STICKS
WHERE DO THEY LIVE
LEO
A WISE GUY EH? SWORD
FAT RAT?
DONNIE
THINKS HE'S SOOO SMART!!! BIG STICK
HYPNOTHERAPY
TONY LOU PIZZA
x2 LARGE
THE WORKS
DELIVERY
MIKEY
SMALL, DUMB STICK WITH BALL
HIDDEN CITY!
WHERE? JERSEY?
BBQ
CHAD!

ART BY CHAD THOMAS

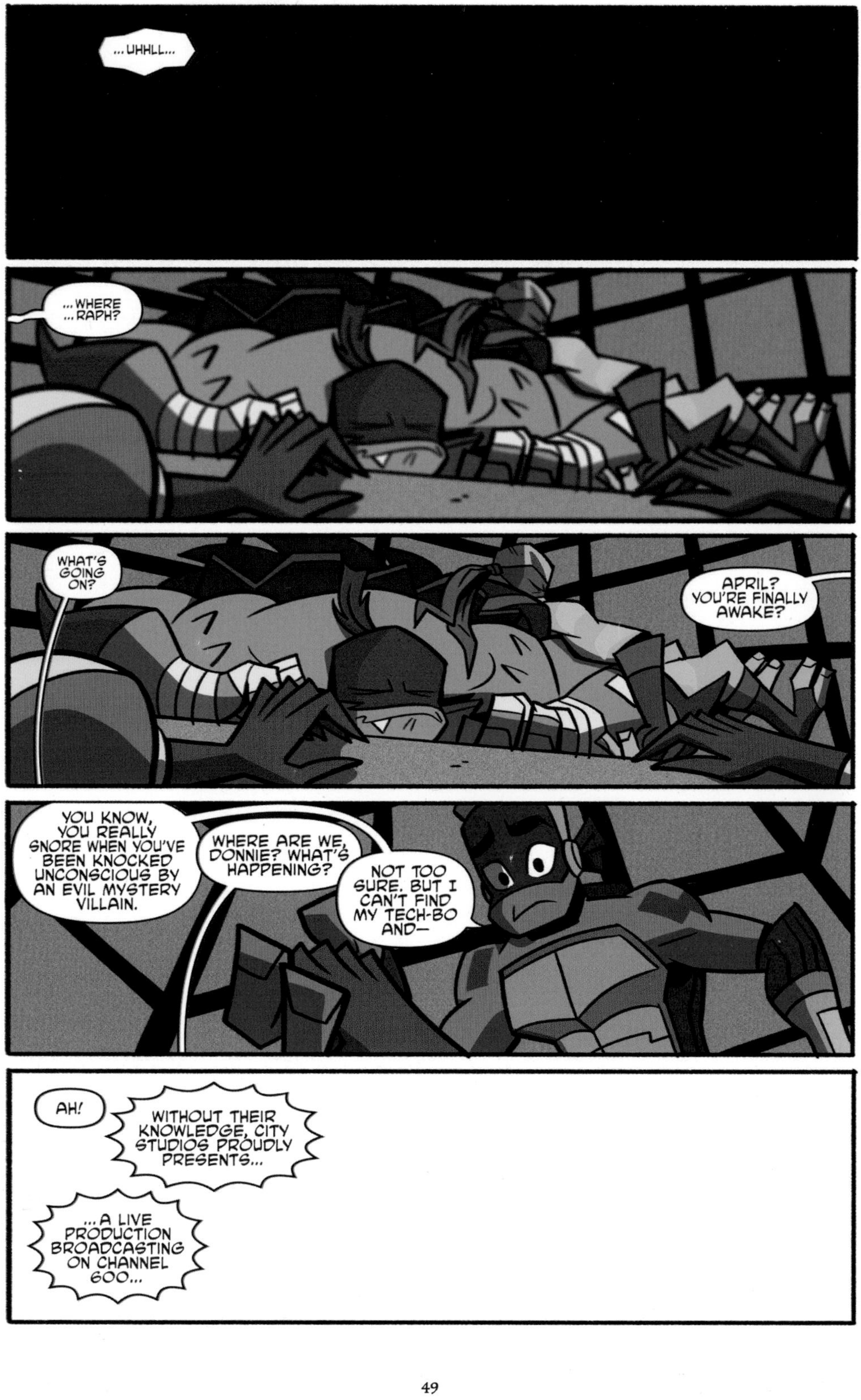
...UHHLL...
...WHERE ...RAPH?
WHAT'S GOING ON?
APRIL? YOU'RE FINALLY AWAKE?
YOU KNOW, YOU REALLY SNORE WHEN YOU'VE BEEN KNOCKED UNCONSCIOUS BY AN EVIL MYSTERY VILLAIN.
WHERE ARE WE, DONNIE? WHAT'S HAPPENING?
NOT TOO SURE. BUT I CAN'T FIND MY TECH-BO AND—
AH!
WITHOUT THEIR KNOWLEDGE, CITY STUDIOS PROUDLY PRESENTS...
...A LIVE PRODUCTION BROADCASTING ON CHANNEL 600...

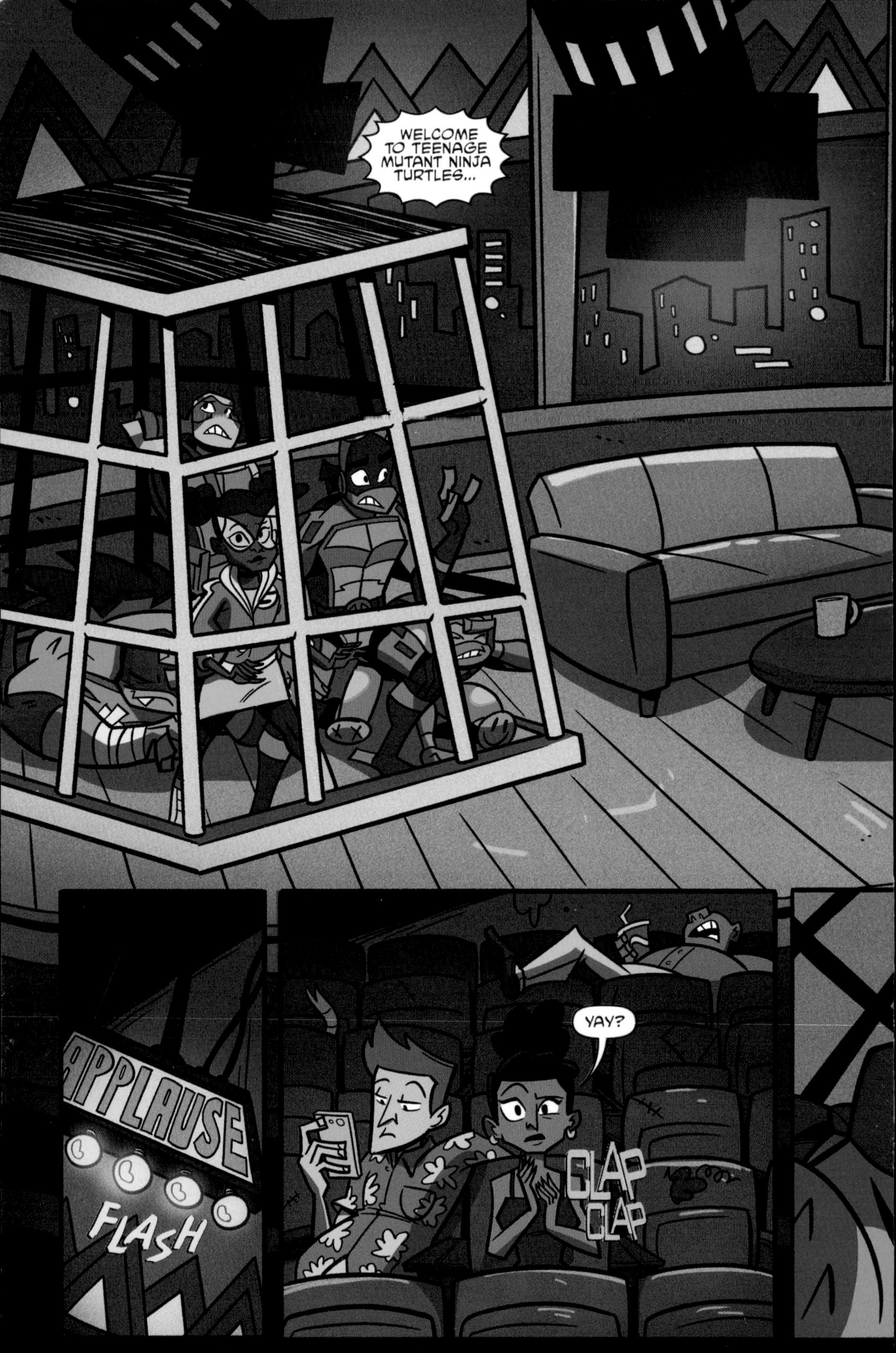
WELCOME TO TEENAGE MUTANT NINJA TURTLES...
APPLAUSE
FLASH
YAY?
CLAP
CLAP

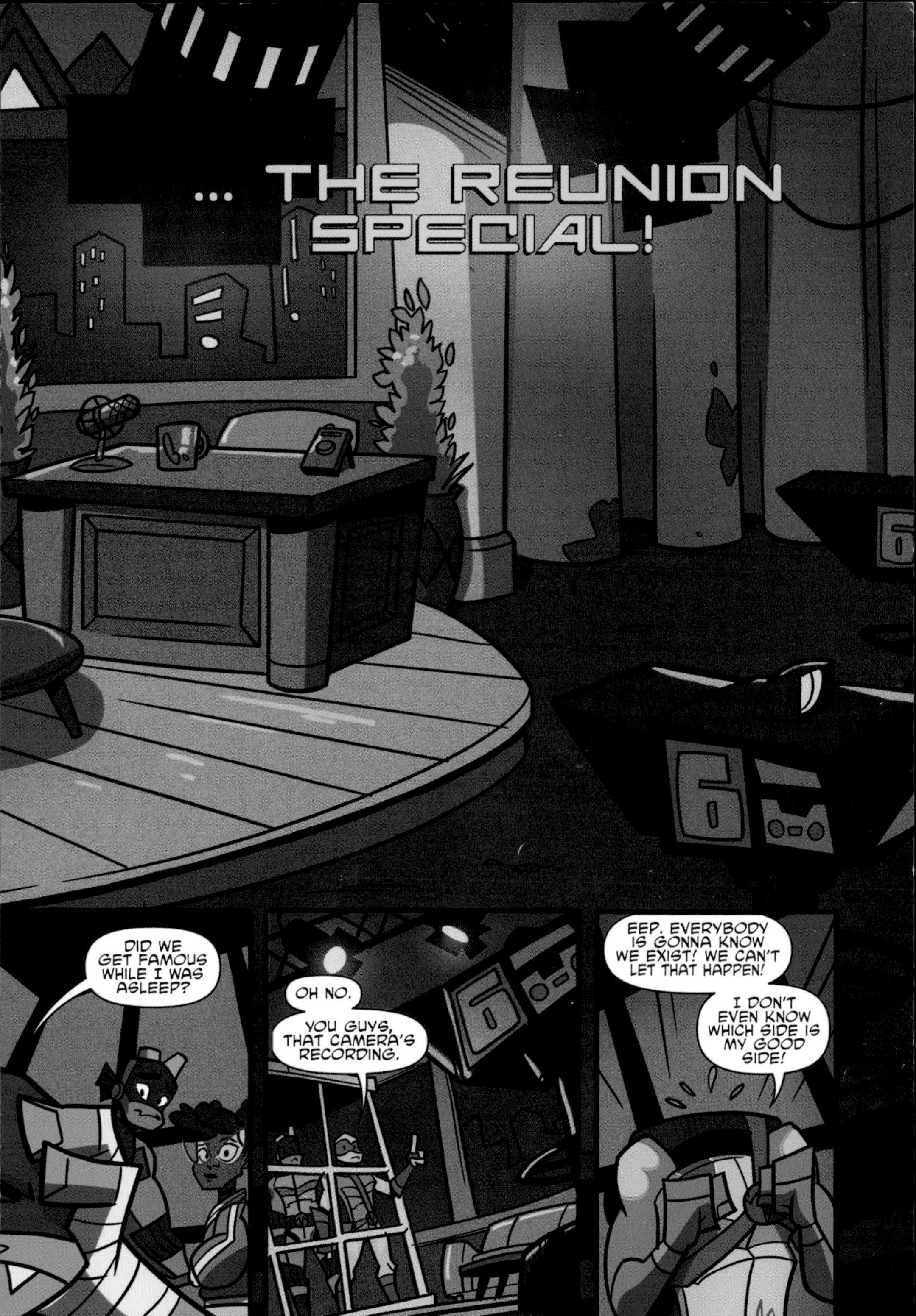
... THE REUNION SPECIAL!
DID WE GET FAMOUS WHILE I WAS ASLEEP?
OH NO.
YOU GUYS, THAT CAMERA'S RECORDING.
EEP. EVERYBODY IS GONNA KNOW WE EXIST! WE CAN'T LET THAT HAPPEN!
I DON'T EVEN KNOW WHICH SIDE IS MY GOOD SIDE!

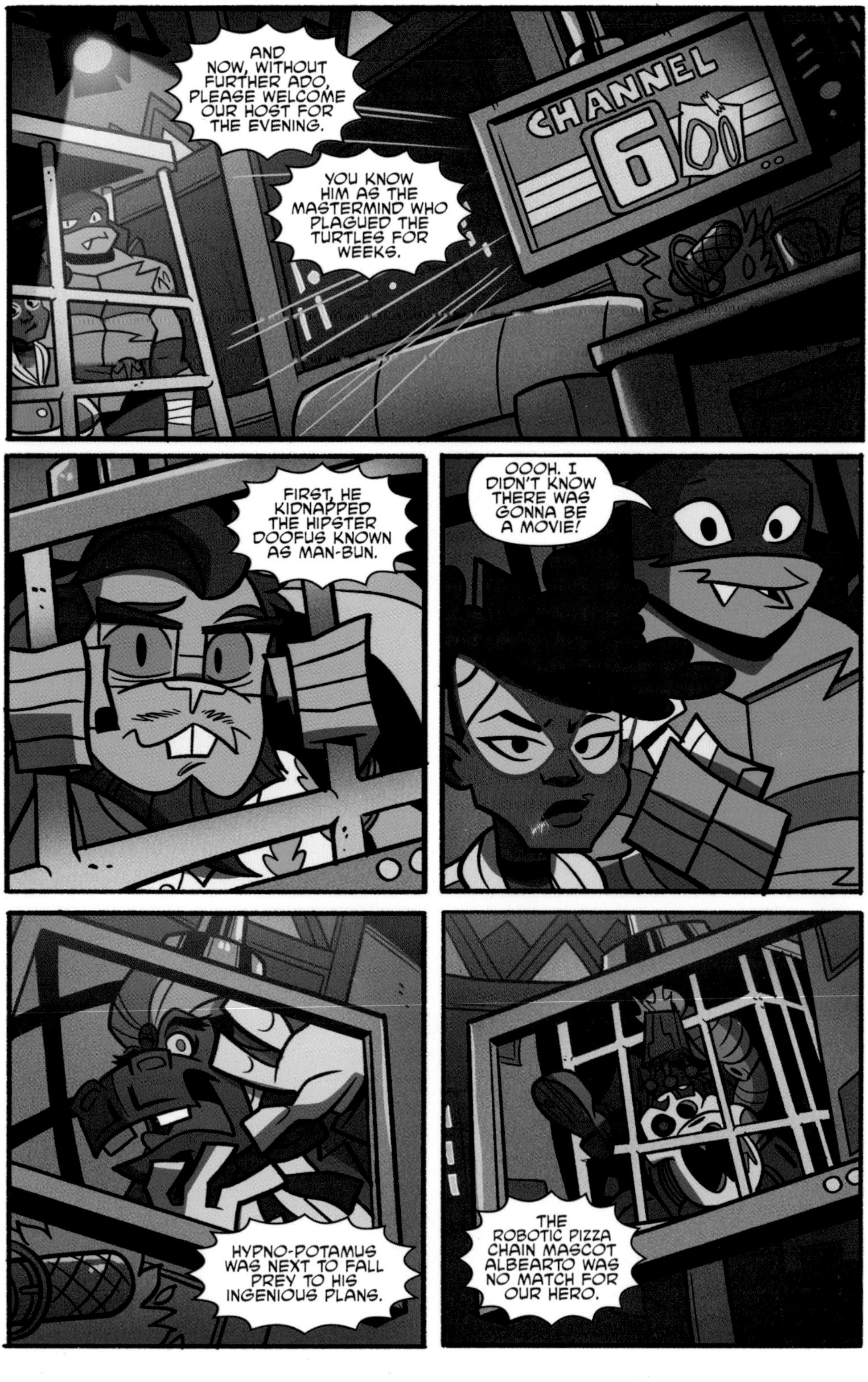
AND NOW, WITHOUT FURTHER ADO, PLEASE WELCOME OUR HOST FOR THE EVENING.
CHANNEL 6
YOU KNOW HIM AS THE MASTERMIND WHO PLAGUED THE TURTLES FOR WEEKS.
FIRST, HE KIDNAPPED THE HIPSTER DOOFUS KNOWN AS MAN-BUN.
OOOH. I DIDN'T KNOW THERE WAS GONNA BE A MOVIE!
HYPNO-POTAMUS WAS NEXT TO FALL PREY TO HIS INGENIOUS PLANS.
THE ROBOTIC PIZZA CHAIN MASCOT ALBEARTO WAS NO MATCH FOR OUR HERO.

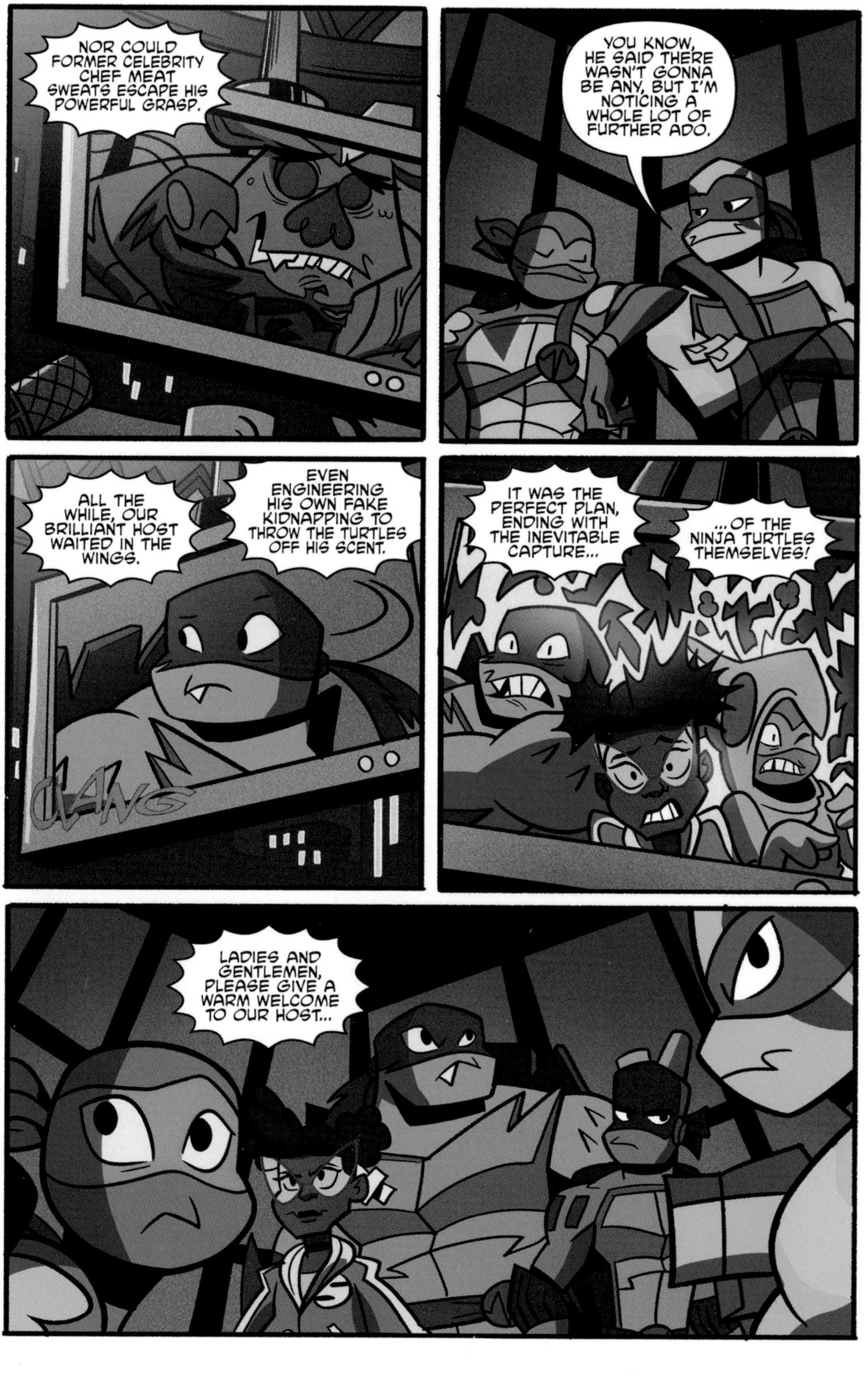
NOR COULD FORMER CELEBRITY CHEF MEAT SWEATS ESCAPE HIS POWERFUL GRASP.
YOU KNOW, HE SAID THERE WASN'T GONNA BE ANY, BUT I'M NOTICING A WHOLE LOT OF FURTHER ADO.
ALL THE WHILE, OUR BRILLIANT HOST WAITED IN THE WINGS.
EVEN ENGINEERING HIS OWN FAKE KIDNAPPING TO THROW THE TURTLES OFF HIS SCENT.
CLANG
IT WAS THE PERFECT PLAN, ENDING WITH THE INEVITABLE CAPTURE...
...OF THE NINJA TURTLES THEMSELVES!
LADIES AND GENTLEMEN, PLEASE GIVE A WARM WELCOME TO OUR HOST...

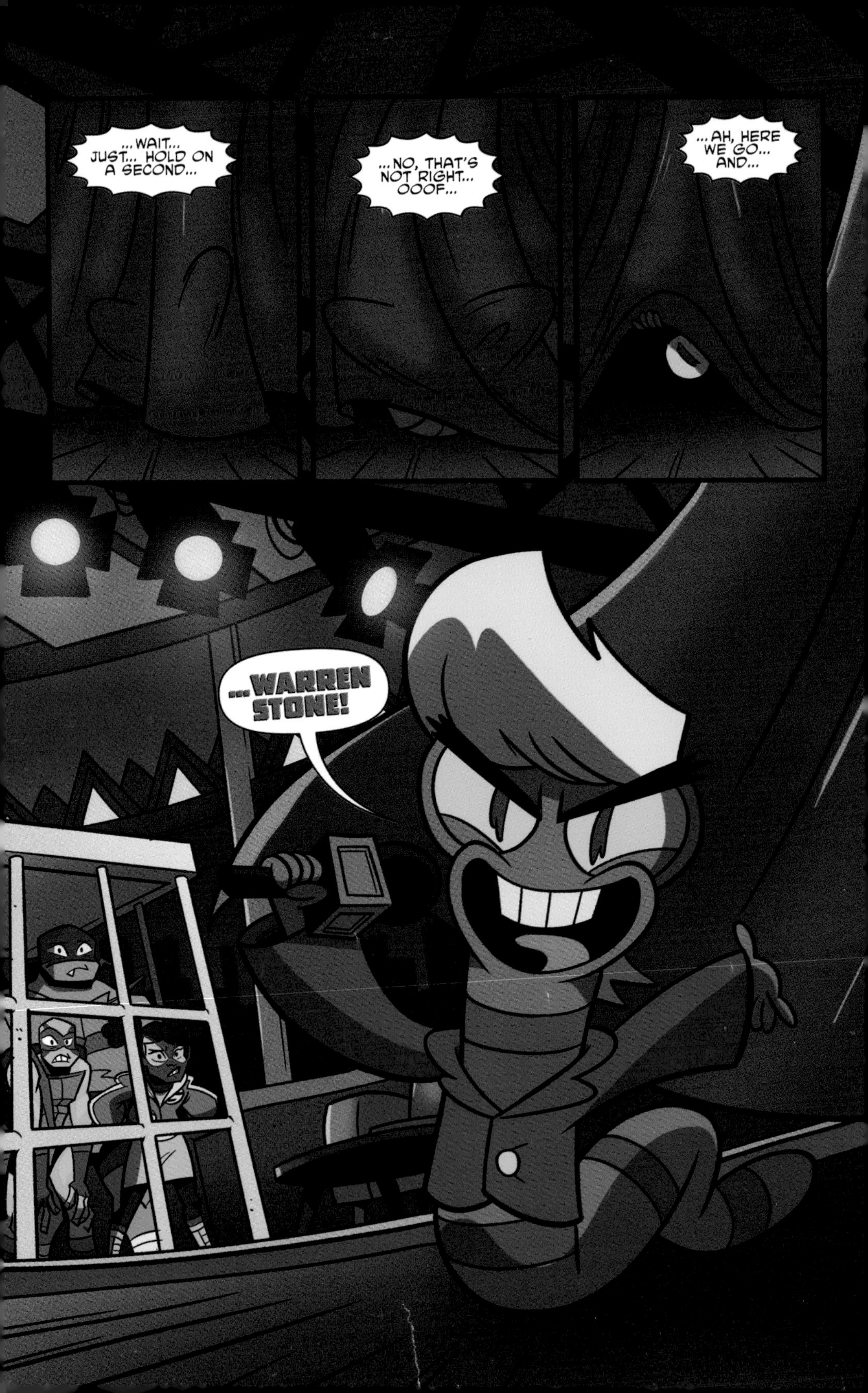
...WAIT... JUST... HOLD ON A SECOND...
...NO, THAT'S NOT RIGHT... OOOF...
...AH, HERE WE GO... AND...
...WARREN STONE!

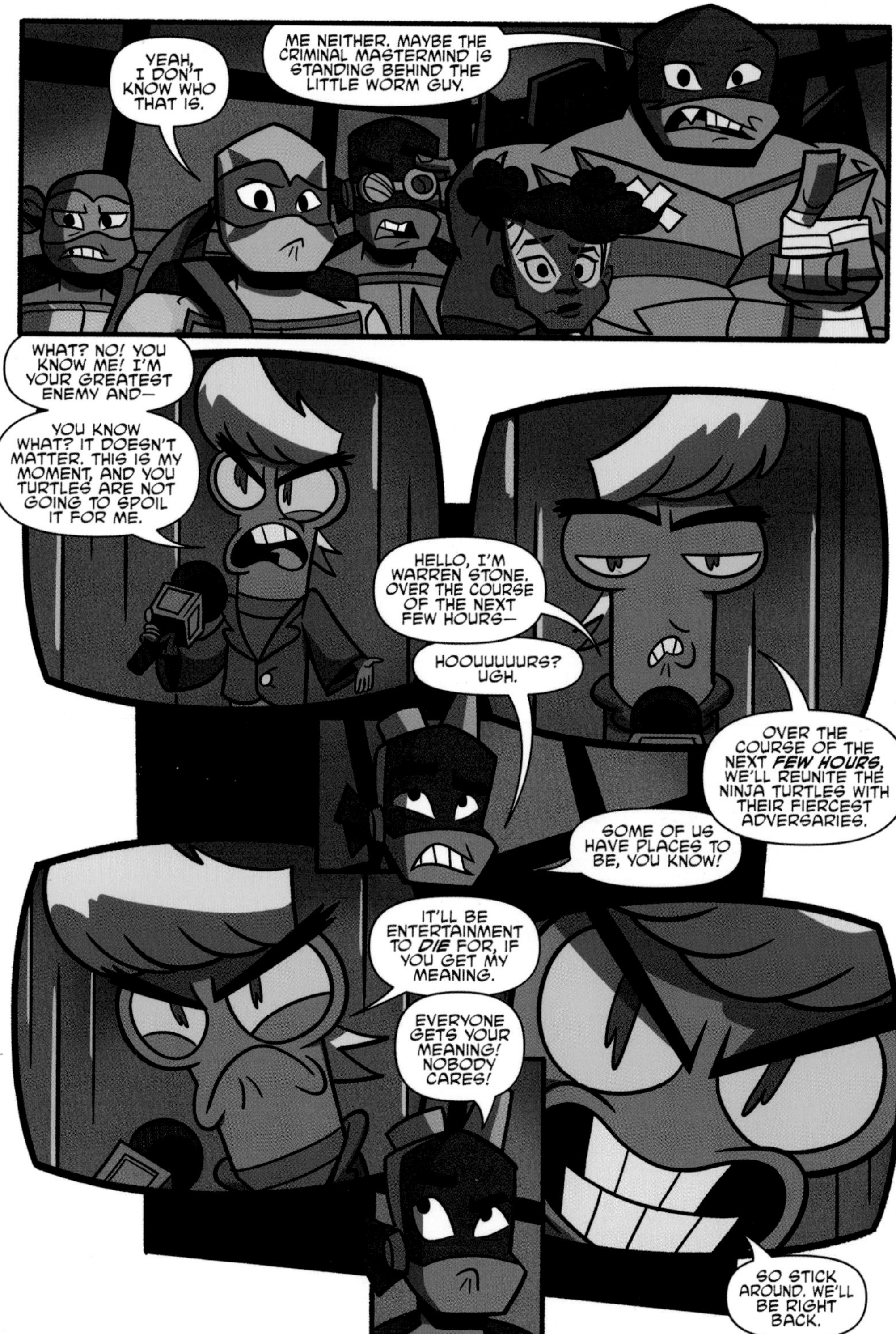

YEAH, I DON'T KNOW WHO THAT IS.
ME NEITHER. MAYBE THE CRIMINAL MASTERMIND IS STANDING BEHIND THE LITTLE WORM GUY.
WHAT? NO! YOU KNOW ME! I'M YOUR GREATEST ENEMY AND—
YOU KNOW WHAT? IT DOESN'T MATTER. THIS IS MY MOMENT, AND YOU TURTLES ARE NOT GOING TO SPOIL IT FOR ME.
HELLO, I'M WARREN STONE. OVER THE COURSE OF THE NEXT FEW HOURS—
HOOUUUUURS? UGH.
OVER THE COURSE OF THE NEXT FEW HOURS, WE'LL REUNITE THE NINJA TURTLES WITH THEIR FIERCEST ADVERSARIES.
SOME OF US HAVE PLACES TO BE, YOU KNOW!
IT'LL BE ENTERTAINMENT TO DIE FOR, IF YOU GET MY MEANING.
EVERYONE GETS YOUR MEANING! NOBODY CARES!
SO STICK AROUND. WE'LL BE RIGHT BACK.

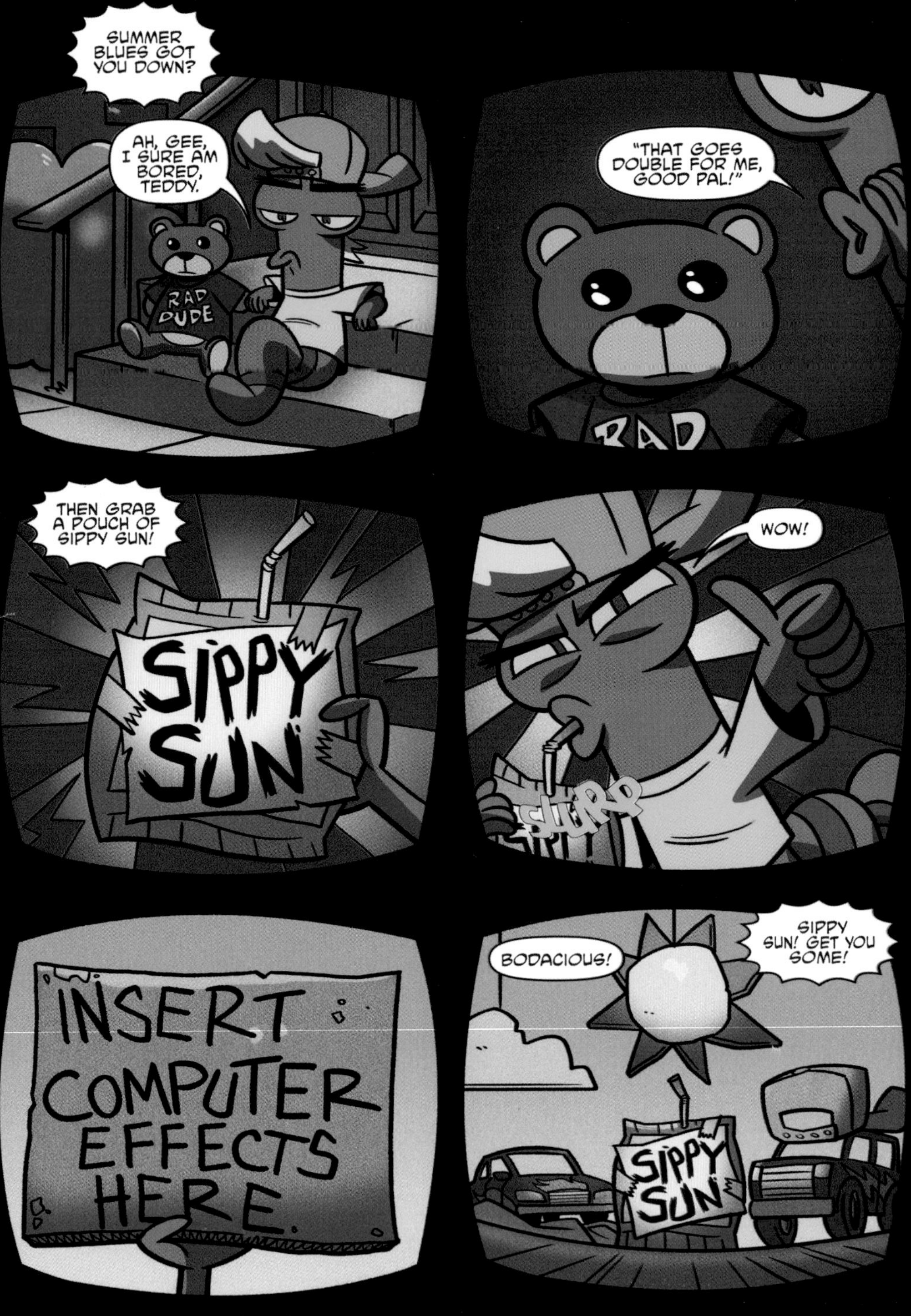
SUMMER BLUES GOT YOU DOWN?
AH, GEE, I SURE AM BORED, TEDDY.
RAD DUDE
"THAT GOES DOUBLE FOR ME, GOOD PAL!"
THEN GRAB A POUCH OF SIPPY SUN!
SIPPY SUN
WOW!
SLURP
INSERT COMPUTER EFFECTS HERE.
BODACIOUS!
SIPPY SUN! GET YOU SOME!
SIPPY SUN

ASK YOUR PHYSICIAN IF SIPPY SUN IS RIGHT FOR YOU.*

*YOUR PHYSICIAN WILL SAY NO.

A PRODUCT OF WARREN STONE, INC.

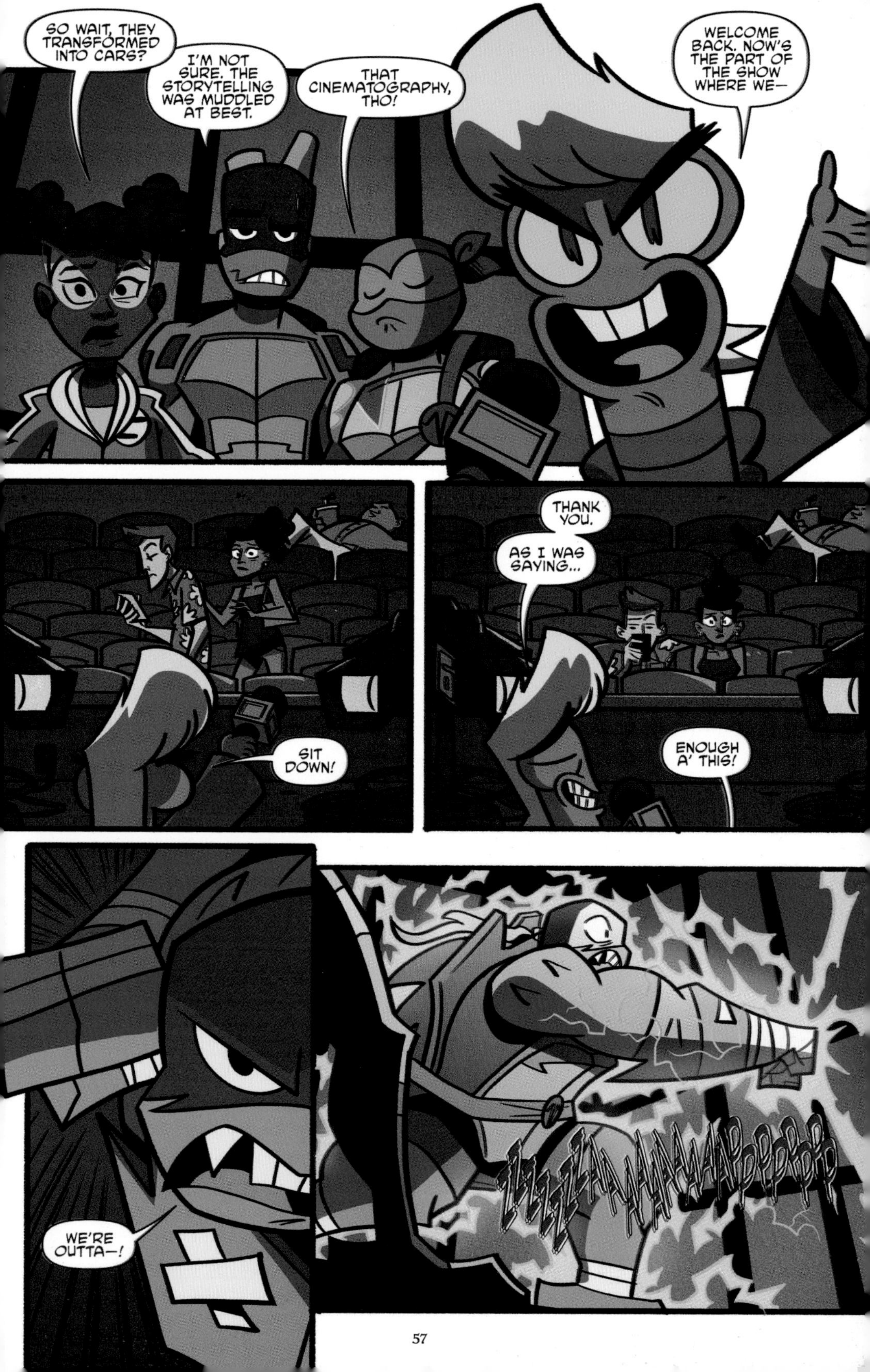
SO WAIT, THEY TRANSFORMED INTO CARS?
I'M NOT SURE. THE STORYTELLING WAS MUDDLED AT BEST.
THAT CINEMATOGRAPHY, THO!
WELCOME BACK. NOW'S THE PART OF THE SHOW WHERE WE—
SIT DOWN!
THANK YOU.
AS I WAS SAYING...
ENOUGH A' THIS!
WE'RE OUTTA—!

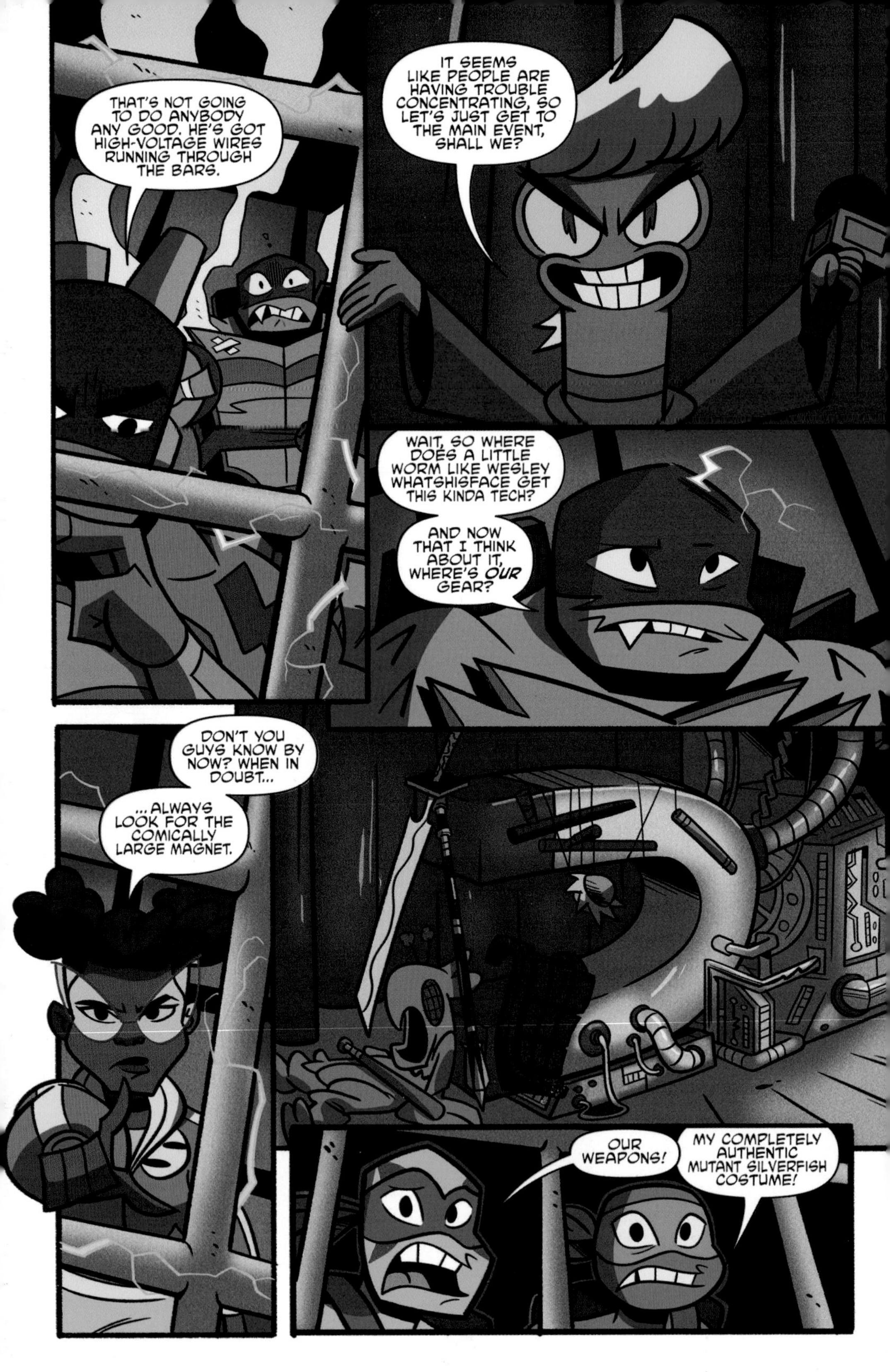
THAT'S NOT GOING TO DO ANYBODY ANY GOOD. HE'S GOT HIGH-VOLTAGE WIRES RUNNING THROUGH THE BARS.
IT SEEMS LIKE PEOPLE ARE HAVING TROUBLE CONCENTRATING, SO LET'S JUST GET TO THE MAIN EVENT, SHALL WE?
WAIT, SO WHERE DOES A LITTLE WORM LIKE WESLEY WHATSHISFACE GET THIS KINDA TECH?
AND NOW THAT I THINK ABOUT IT, WHERE'S *OUR* GEAR?
DON'T YOU GUYS KNOW BY NOW? WHEN IN DOUBT...
...ALWAYS LOOK FOR THE COMICALLY LARGE MAGNET.
OUR WEAPONS!
MY COMPLETELY AUTHENTIC MUTANT SILVERFISH COSTUME!

YOU ALL SHOULD RECOGNIZE THESE FRIENDLY FACES, EVEN IF YOU HAVE THE MEMORY RETENTION OF A GOLDFISH.
PUT YOUR HANDS TOGETHER FOR THE FEARSOME FOURSOME...
HYPNO-POTAMUS!
MAN-BUN!
MEAT SWEATS!
ALBEARTO!
...
YEAH.
WHAT DONNIE SAID.

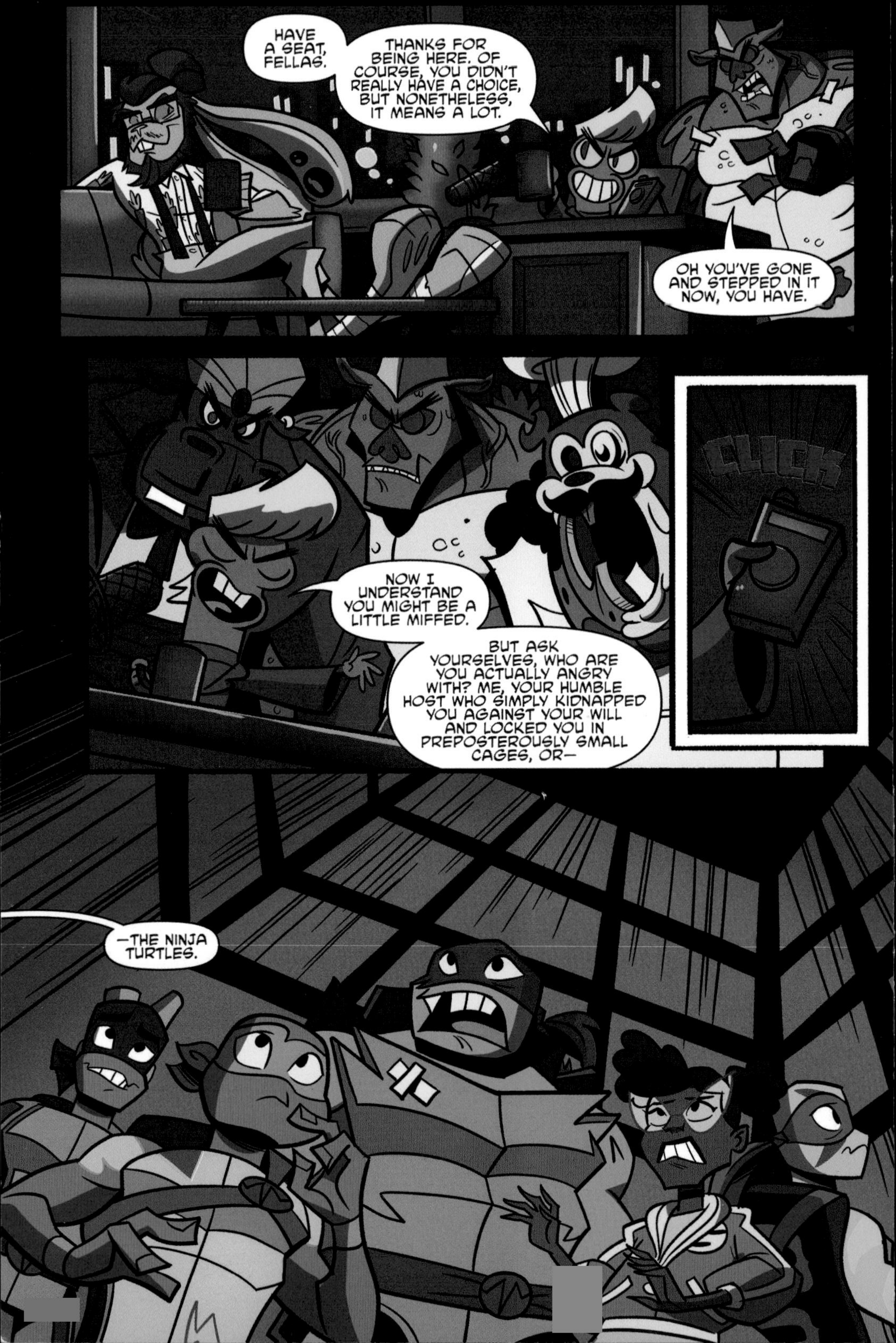
HAVE A SEAT, FELLAS.
THANKS FOR BEING HERE. OF COURSE, YOU DIDN'T REALLY HAVE A CHOICE, BUT NONETHELESS, IT MEANS A LOT.
OH YOU'VE GONE AND STEPPED IN IT NOW, YOU HAVE.
CLICK
NOW I UNDERSTAND YOU MIGHT BE A LITTLE MIFFED.
BUT ASK YOURSELVES, WHO ARE YOU ACTUALLY ANGRY WITH? ME, YOUR HUMBLE HOST WHO SIMPLY KIDNAPPED YOU AGAINST YOUR WILL AND LOCKED YOU IN PREPOSTEROUSLY SMALL CAGES, OR—
—THE NINJA TURTLES.

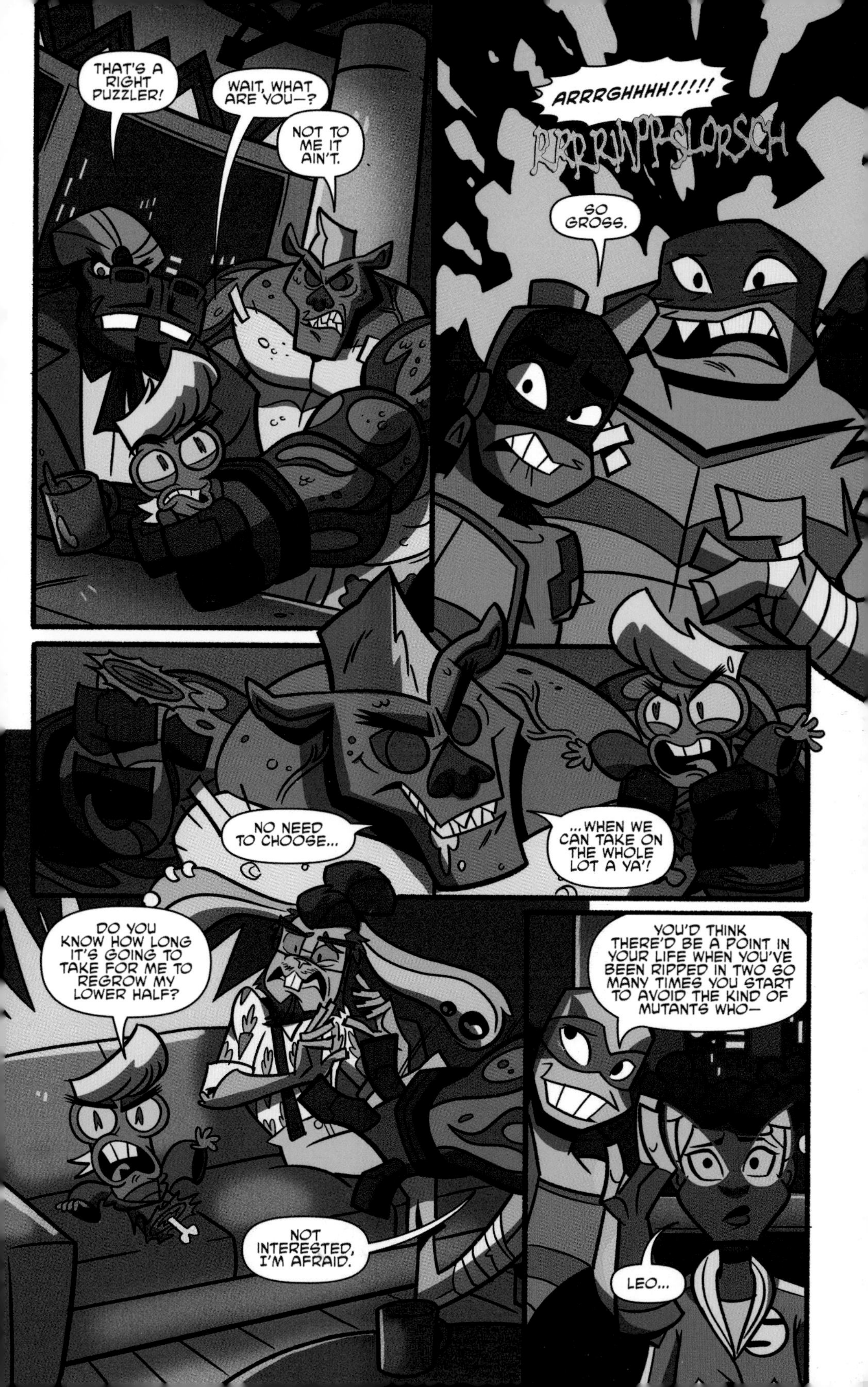
THAT'S A RIGHT PUZZLER!
WAIT, WHAT ARE YOU—?
NOT TO ME IT AIN'T.
ARRRGHHHH!!!!!
RRRRIIPPPSLORSCH
SO GROSS.
NO NEED TO CHOOSE...
...WHEN WE CAN TAKE ON THE WHOLE LOT A YA'!
DO YOU KNOW HOW LONG IT'S GOING TO TAKE FOR ME TO REGROW MY LOWER HALF?
NOT INTERESTED, I'M AFRAID.
YOU'D THINK THERE'D BE A POINT IN YOUR LIFE WHEN YOU'VE BEEN RIPPED IN TWO SO MANY TIMES YOU START TO AVOID THE KIND OF MUTANTS WHO—
LEO...

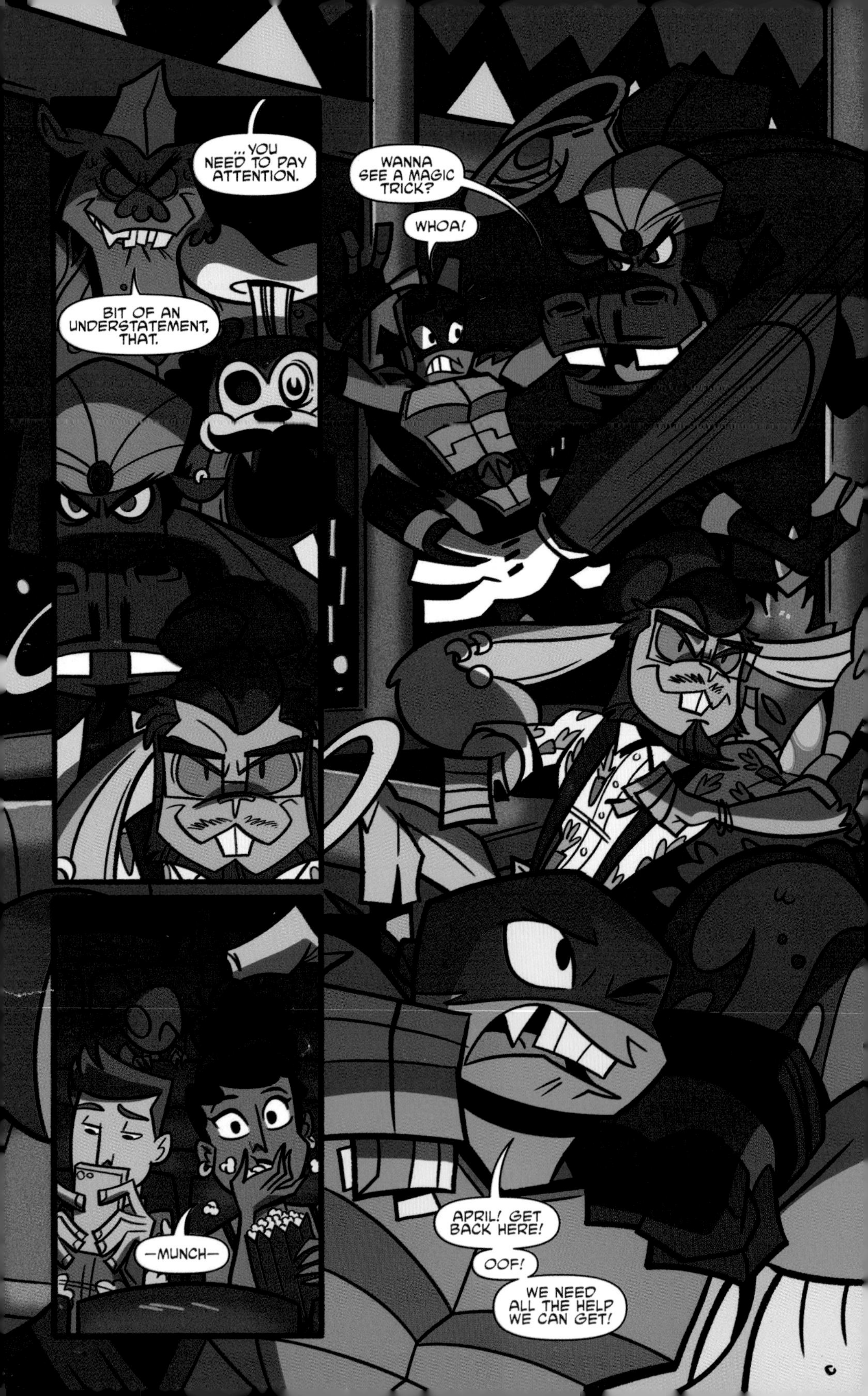
...YOU NEED TO PAY ATTENTION.
BIT OF AN UNDERSTATEMENT, THAT.
WANNA SEE A MAGIC TRICK?
WHOA!
—MUNCH—
APRIL! GET BACK HERE!
OOF!
WE NEED ALL THE HELP WE CAN GET!

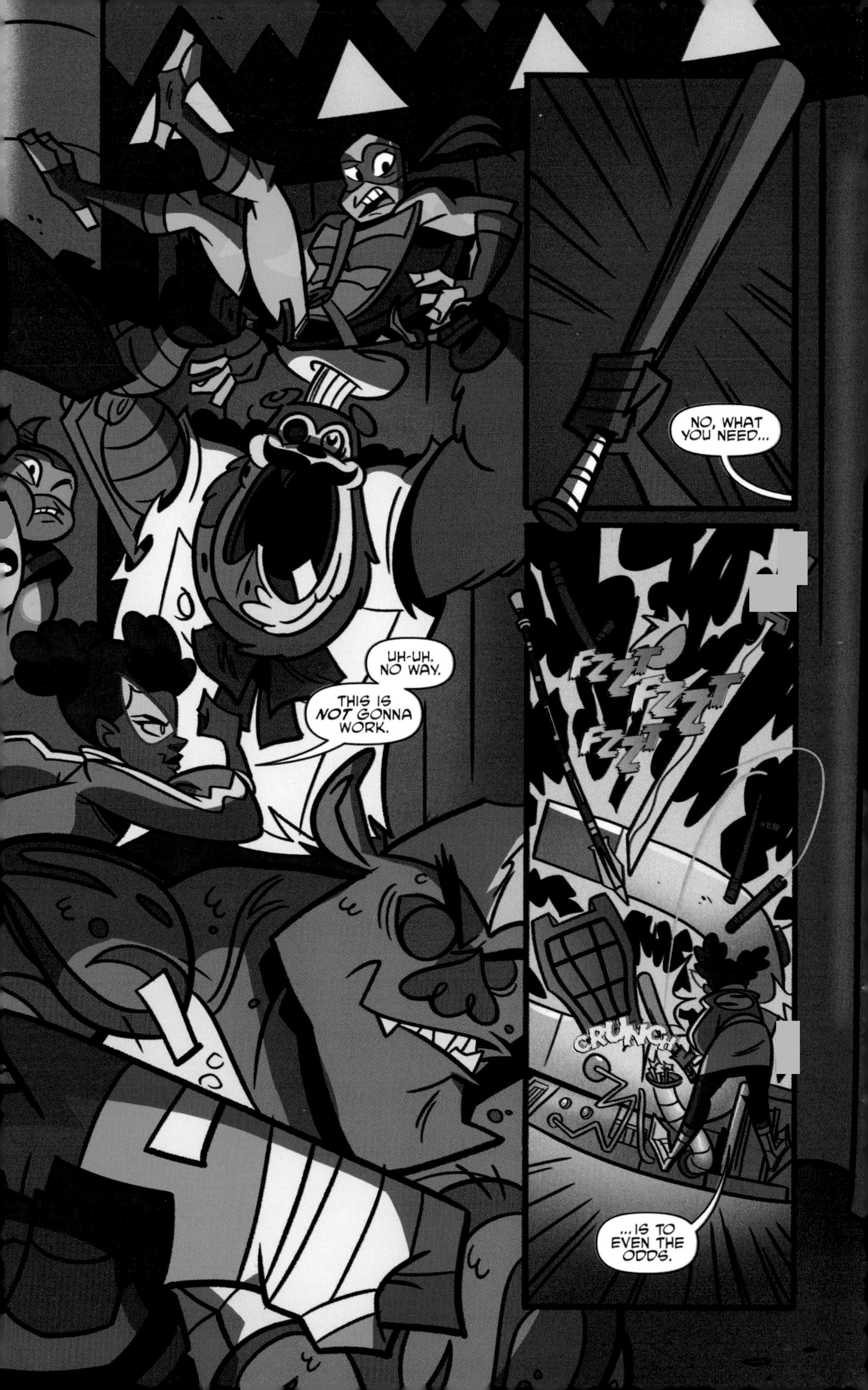
UH-UH. NO WAY.
THIS IS *NOT* GONNA WORK.
NO, WHAT YOU NEED...
FZZT
FZZT
FZZT
CRUNCH
...IS TO EVEN THE ODDS.

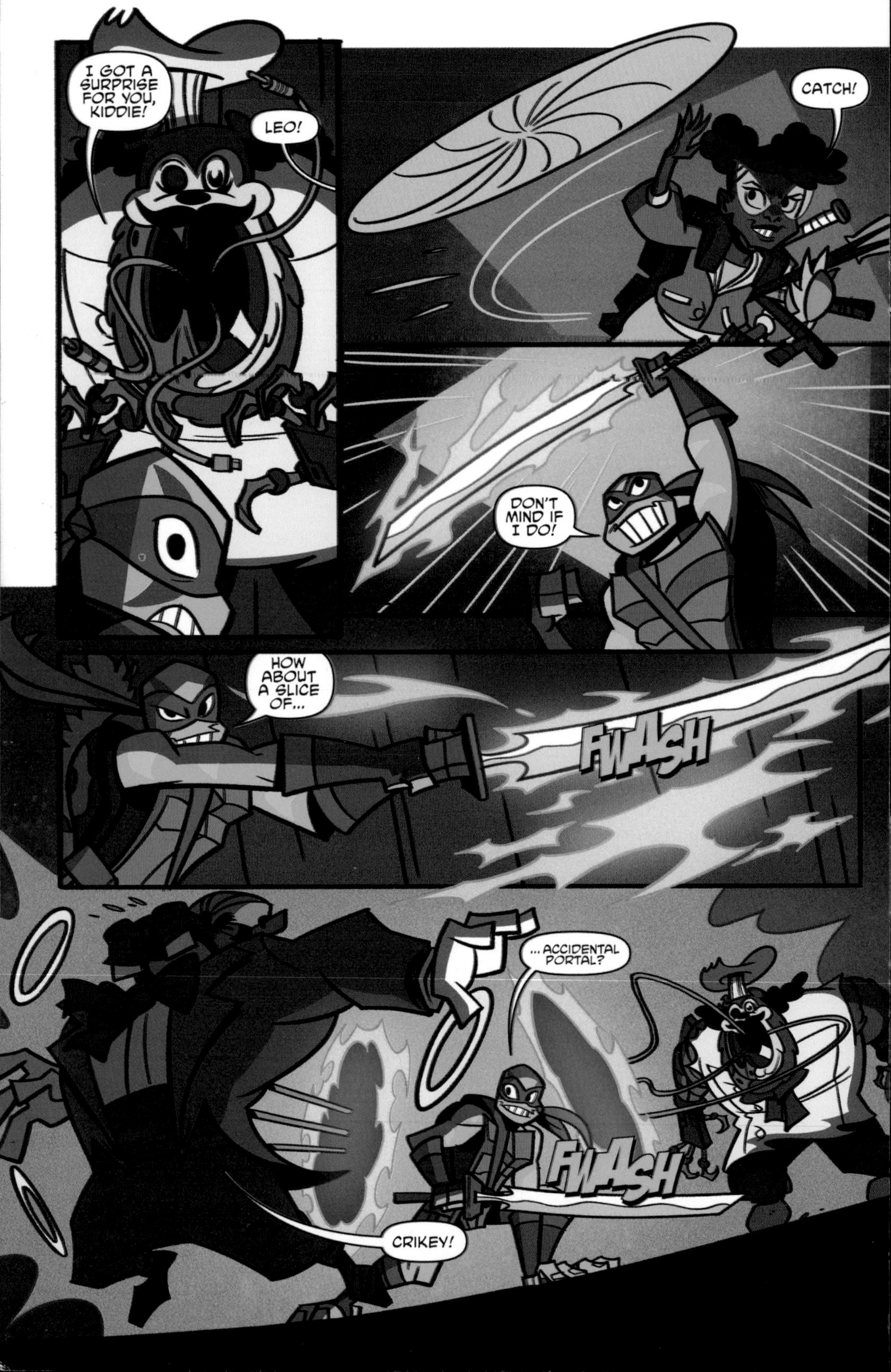
I GOT A SURPRISE FOR YOU, KIDDIE!
LEO!
CATCH!
DON'T MIND IF I DO!
HOW ABOUT A SLICE OF...
FWASH
...ACCIDENTAL PORTAL?
FWASH
CRIKEY!

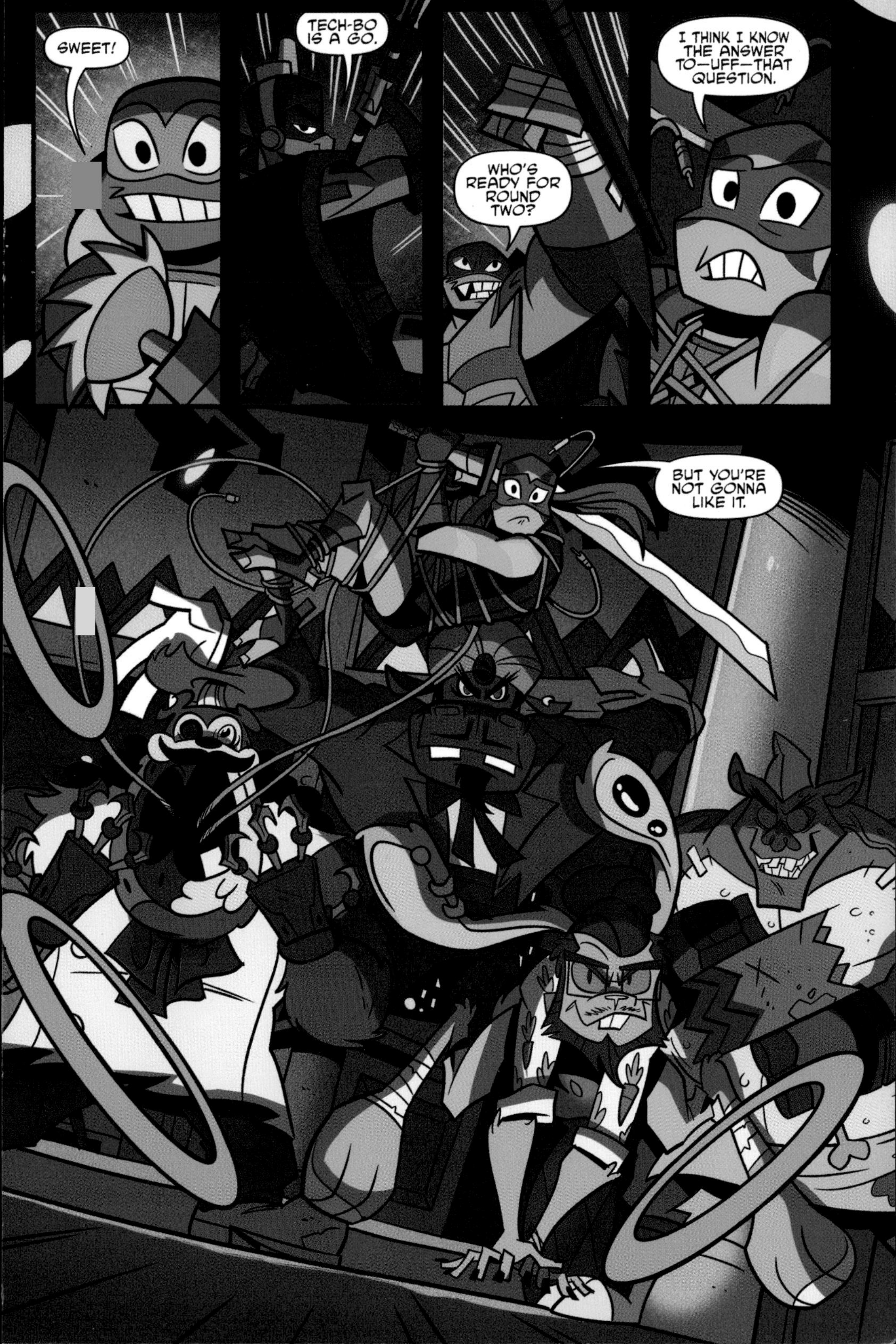
SWEET!
TECH-BO IS A GO.
WHO'S READY FOR ROUND TWO?
I THINK I KNOW THE ANSWER TO—UFF—THAT QUESTION.
BUT YOU'RE NOT GONNA LIKE IT.

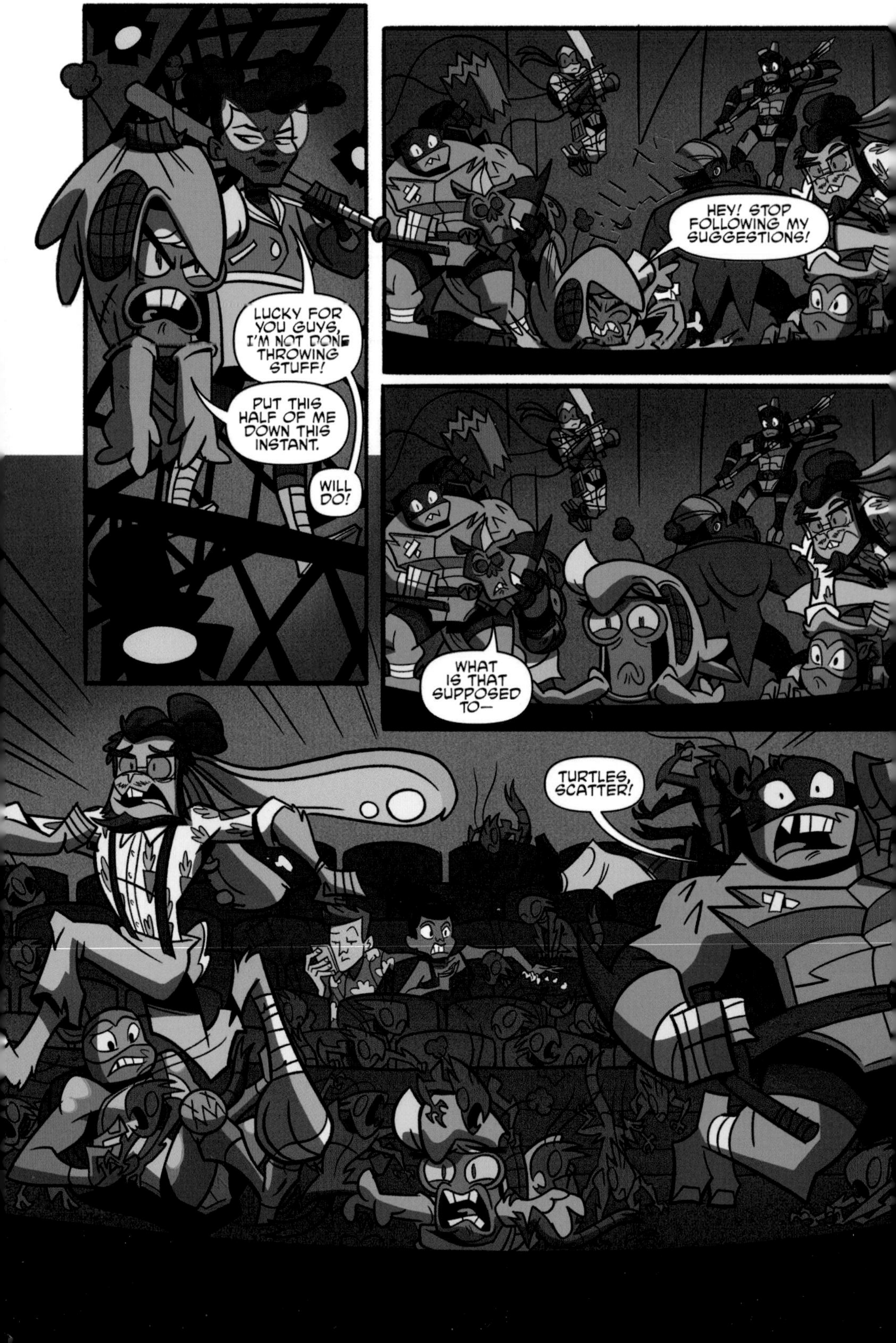
LUCKY FOR YOU GUYS, I'M NOT DONE THROWING STUFF!
PUT THIS HALF OF ME DOWN THIS INSTANT.
WILL DO!
HEY! STOP FOLLOWING MY SUGGESTIONS!
WHAT IS THAT SUPPOSED TO—
TURTLES, SCATTER!

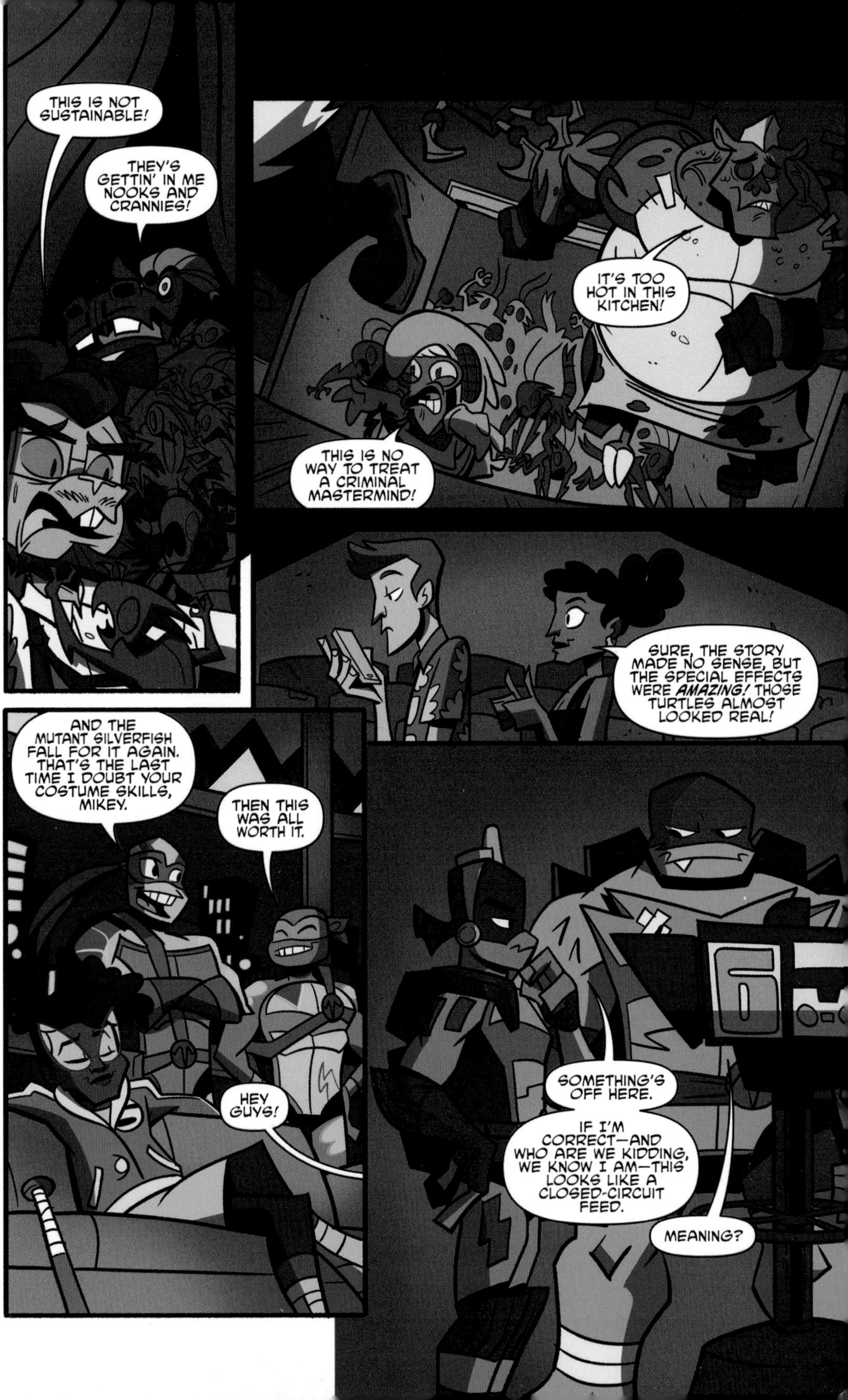
THIS IS NOT SUSTAINABLE!
THEY'S GETTIN' IN ME NOOKS AND CRANNIES!
IT'S TOO HOT IN THIS KITCHEN!
THIS IS NO WAY TO TREAT A CRIMINAL MASTERMIND!
SURE, THE STORY MADE NO SENSE, BUT THE SPECIAL EFFECTS WERE *AMAZING!* THOSE TURTLES ALMOST LOOKED REAL!
AND THE MUTANT SILVERFISH FALL FOR IT AGAIN. THAT'S THE LAST TIME I DOUBT YOUR COSTUME SKILLS, MIKEY.
THEN THIS WAS ALL WORTH IT.
HEY GUYS!
SOMETHING'S OFF HERE.
IF I'M CORRECT—AND WHO ARE WE KIDDING, WE KNOW I AM—THIS LOOKS LIKE A CLOSED-CIRCUIT FEED.
MEANING?

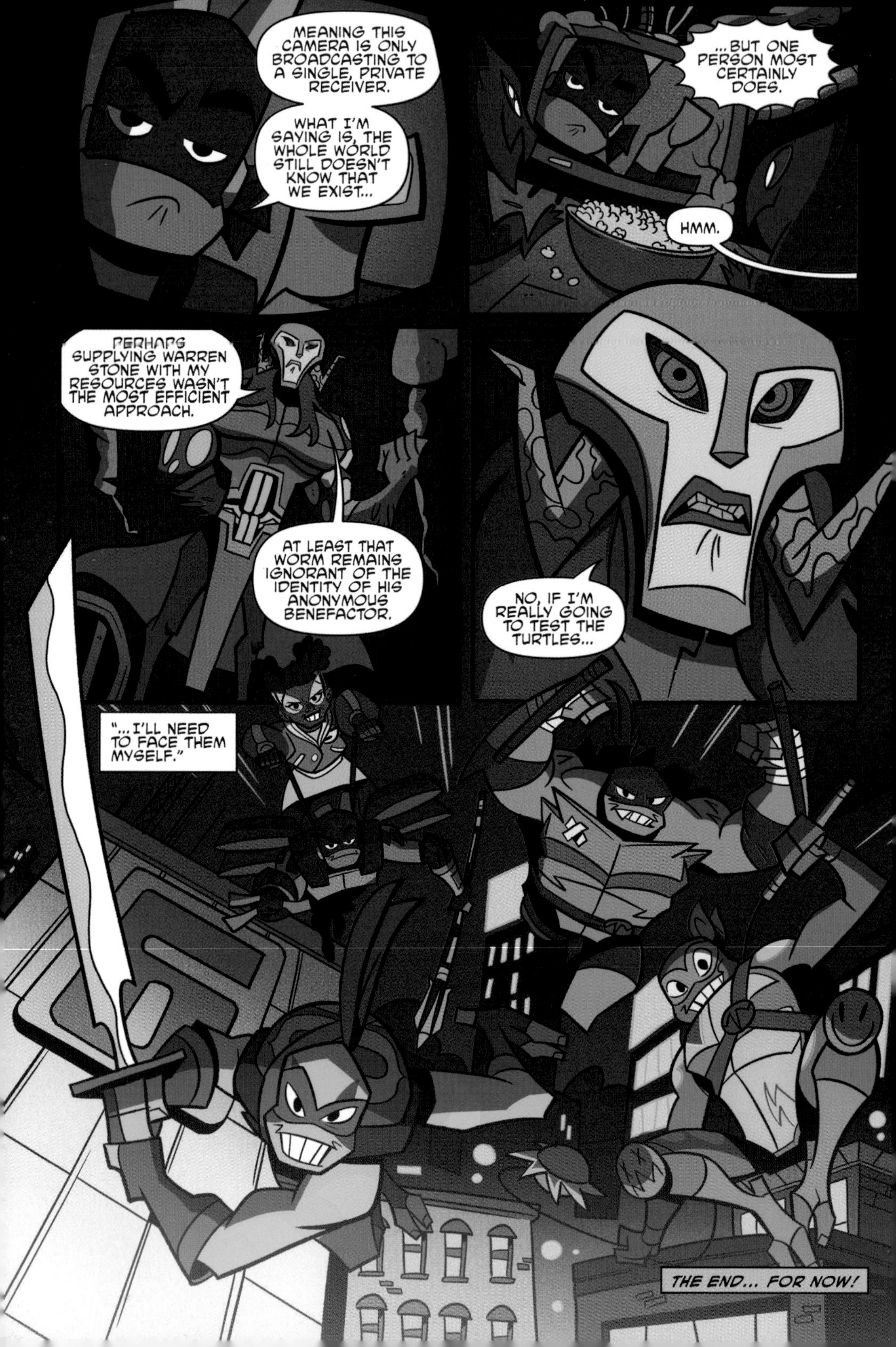
MEANING THIS CAMERA IS ONLY BROADCASTING TO A SINGLE, PRIVATE RECEIVER.
WHAT I'M SAYING IS, THE WHOLE WORLD STILL DOESN'T KNOW THAT WE EXIST...
...BUT ONE PERSON MOST CERTAINLY DOES.
HMM.
PERHAPS SUPPLYING WARREN STONE WITH MY RESOURCES WASN'T THE MOST EFFICIENT APPROACH.
AT LEAST THAT WORM REMAINS IGNORANT OF THE IDENTITY OF HIS ANONYMOUS BENEFACTOR.
NO, IF I'M REALLY GOING TO TEST THE TURTLES...
"...I'LL NEED TO FACE THEM MYSELF."
THE END... FOR NOW!

WARREN
STONE

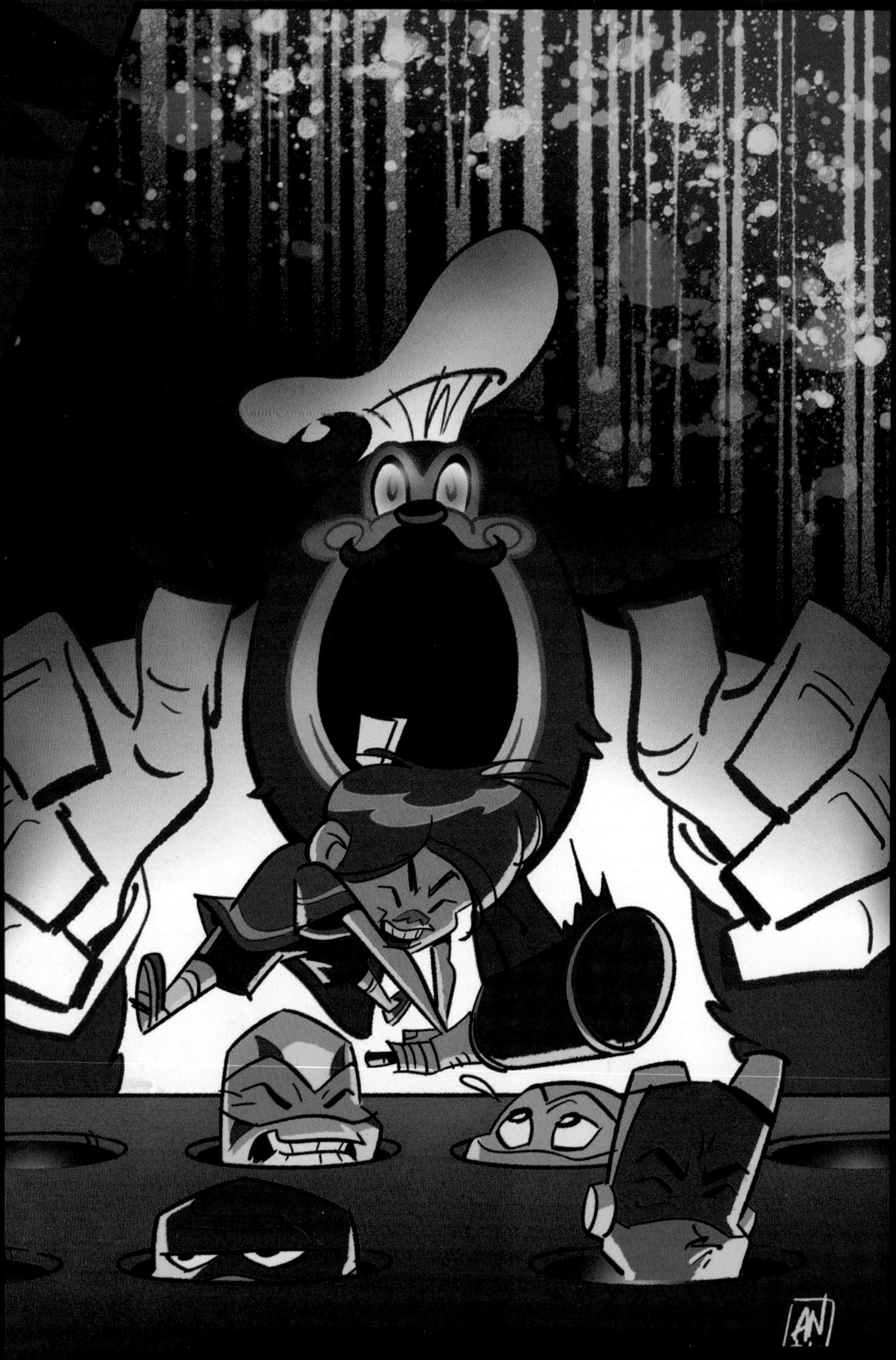

ART BY ANDY SURIANO

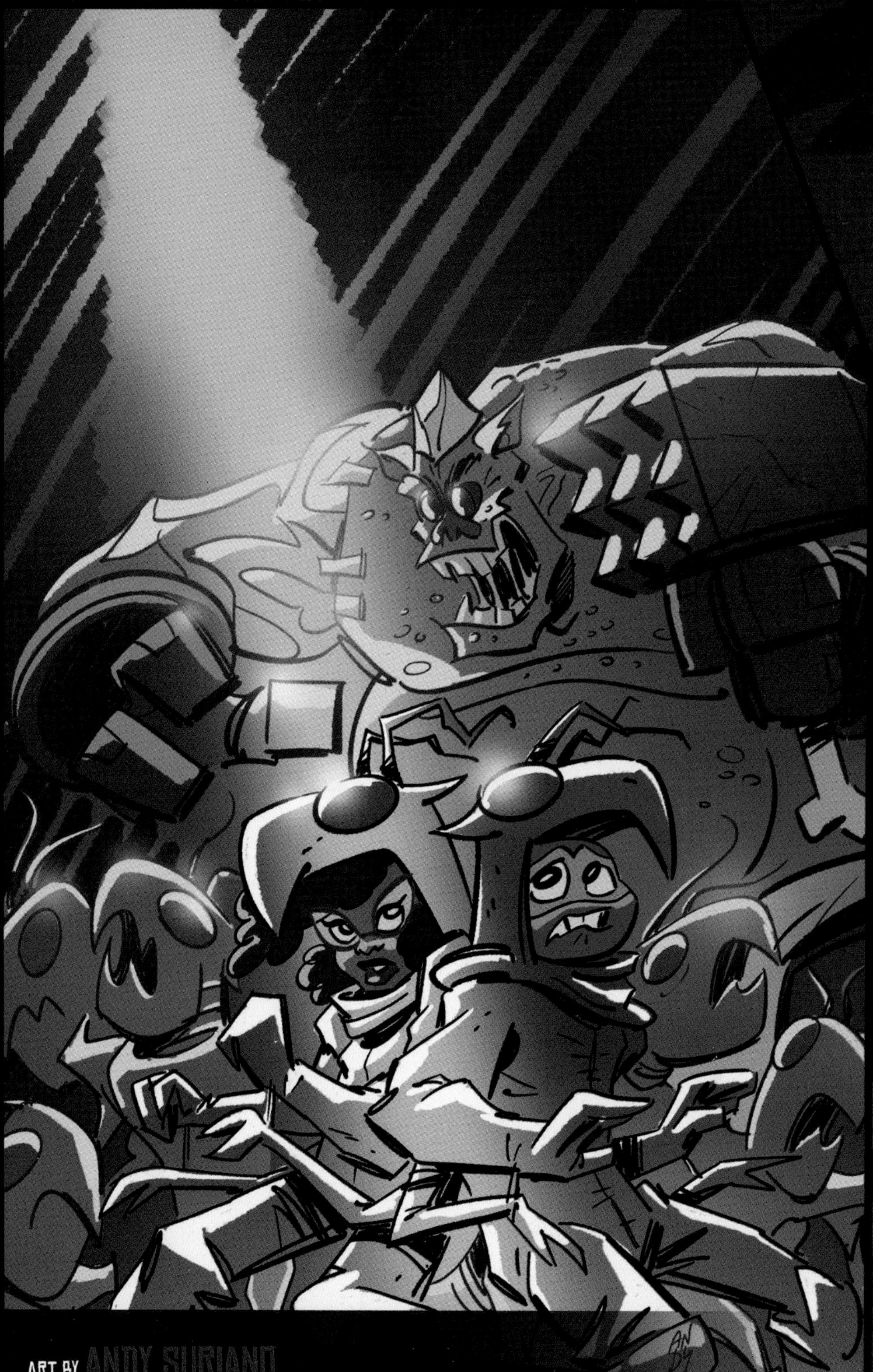

ART BY ANDY SURIANO

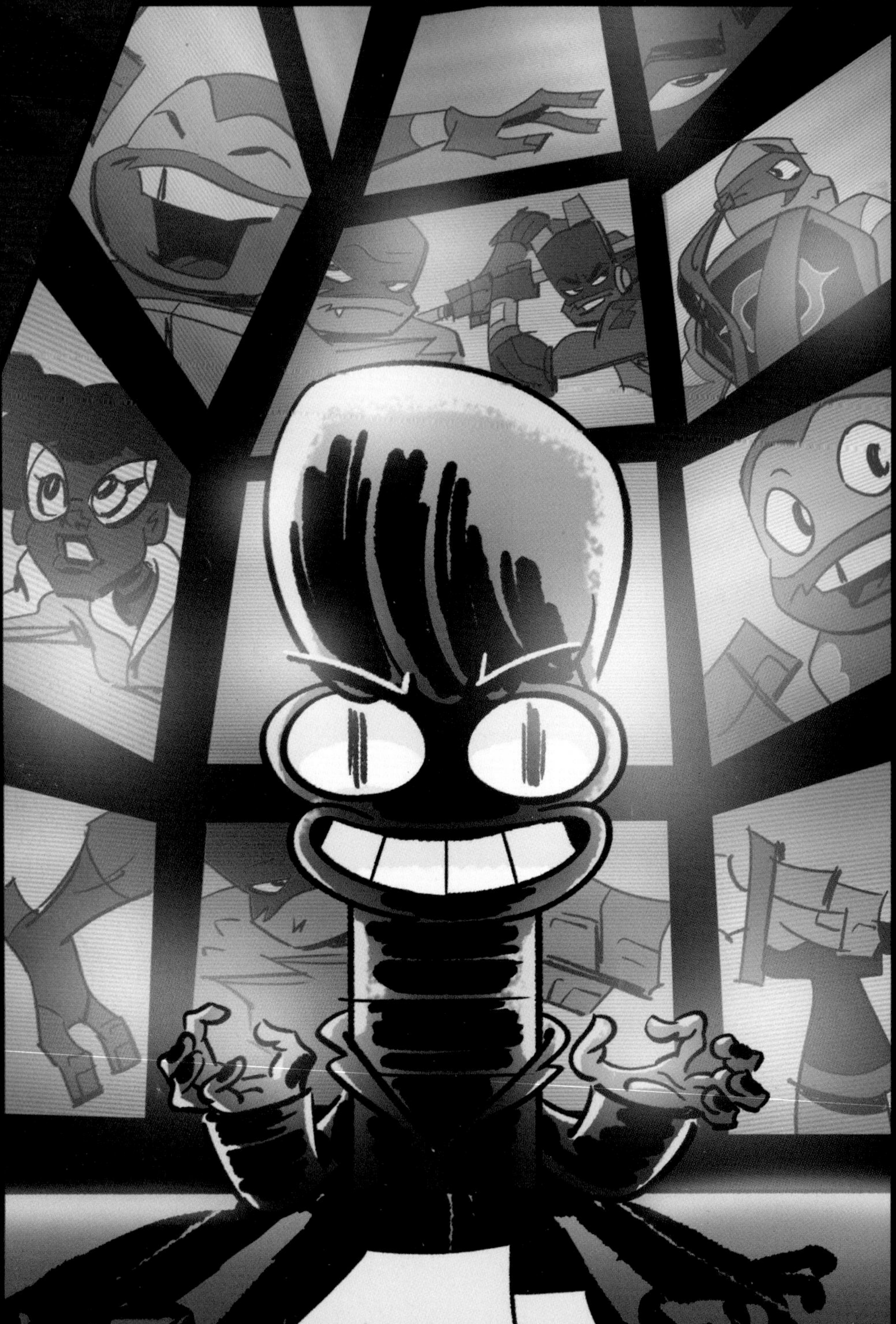

ART BY ANDY SURIANO